SACRAMENTO PUBLIC LIBRARY
828 "I" Street
Sacramento, CA 95814
08/15

A King Production presents…

D0756839

MAFIA Princess

To Love, Honor and Betray PART 3

A NOVEL

JOY DEJA KING
AND CHRIS BOOKER

This novel is a work of fiction. Any references to real people, events, establishments, or locales are intended only to give the fiction a sense of reality and authenticity. Other names, characters, and incidents occurring in the work are either the product of the author's imagination or are used fictitiously, as those fictionalized events and incidents that involve real persons. Any character that happens to share the name of a person who is an acquaintance of the author, past or present, is purely coincidental and is in no way intended to be an actual account involving that person.

ISBN 13: 978-0986004506

ISBN 10: 0986004502

Cover concept by Joy Deja King & www.MarionDesigns.com
Cover layout and graphic design by www.MarionDesigns.com
Cover Model: Shanel Nelson
Typesetting: Keith Saunders
Editor: Linda Williams

Library of Congress Cataloging-in-Publication Data;
A King Production
Mafia Princess Part 3 by: Joy Deja King/Chris Booker
For complete Library of Congress Copyright info visit;
www.joydejaking.com

A KING PRODUCTION

A King Production
P.O. Box 912, Collierville, TN 38027

A King Production and the above portrayal log are trademarks of
A King Production LLC

Copyright © 2012 by A King Production LLC. All rights reserved. No part of this book may be reproduced in any form without the permission from the publisher, except by reviewer who may quote brief passage to be printed in a newspaper or magazine.

Dedication

This Book is Dedicated To My:
Family, Readers and Supporters.
I LOVE you guys so much. Please believe that!!

—Joy Deja King

A KING PRODUCTION
MAFIA
Princess
PART 3
To Love, Honor and Betray
A NOVEL
JOY DEJA KING
AND CHRIS BOOKER

Chapter 1

Cars were lined up bumper to bumper as they drove slowly down 125th Street in Harlem for Semaj's funeral. The last time anything this big happened was when Biggie died, and even now there were still more people attending Semaj's final ride through the city. There were people there that weren't family or friends of Semaj, but they were supporting the ones that did know her. At least one member out of the families of the 16 Tent attended, and Valentina was there for Colombia.

Gio, along with Sosa drove in the first limo right behind the hearse. Gio was sick to death. He couldn't bear to look at anybody, and it was hard for him to hold back his tears.

"Don't worry, Gio. I'ma find out who did this to Maj and I'ma kill them and everybody that exists in their family!" Marcela cried lightly as she looked out of the window at the people standing outside of the church when they pulled up.

"I failed. What made me any better than her

father? I couldn't protect her. I couldn't protect my only grandchild!" Gio whined, damn near ready to cry himself. All he could do was think about her cold body lying in the morgue on that steel table. He felt totally responsible for everything that happened, being as though he was the one that sought Semaj out and brought her into the family. He took her away from the possibility of becoming an actress and doing something good with her life. All these years he had waited to see her, and now he was burying her.

There wasn't a dry face in the building as everyone walked through the door and took their seats for the viewing. Security was extremely tight, and every last soul had to walk through a metal detector placed at the front door. The only people that were armed were Emilia, who stood posted by the door, and Marcela, who stood off to the side close to Gio and the rest of the immediate family.

The sounds of crying filled the church, and for a minute Gio didn't want to be the boss of the family. He wanted to weep at his granddaughter's wake. He wanted to shed a few tears, but doing so would only show a sign of weakness that every wolf in the building wanted to see.

"Maj! Maj!" Sosa cried out and buried her head in LuLu's chest as she thought about the good times she and Semaj had.

The funeral was closed casket due to the blast that took off half of Semaj's face, so the only thing standing in front of the altar was a giant picture of her when she was younger. This was the toughest pill anybody in the family had to swallow after the death of Kasey, her mother. Some people had to get up and leave because they couldn't stay and go through the pain. The blow overall was devastating, and was the beginning of the Milano Family's downfall.

The cool breeze from the ocean water wafted through the window of the massive ocean view bedroom. The large white canopy draped over the bed and the sounds of the ocean pierced her ears as she tried to wake up. She opened, and then closed her eyes as she went in and out of consciousness. Every time she opened her eyes, she would see Qua standing over her. Although unable to say a word, or even maintain consciousness for that matter, she felt safe and secure with him by her side.

"Kola, do you know what time Ox will be back?" Qua asked the head maid as she brought some fresh towels to the room.

"Me not know. He come and go when he please," she said, continuing her daily routine. "If you want, I can call 'im fer ya."

"Nah, its cool, Kola. I'll try calling him again myself in a couple minutes," he responded, looking down at Semaj's badly scarred face.

There wasn't much Qua could do for her, and until

Ox got back home, she wouldn't be able to see the doctor. The local doctor was the one that patched her up, but nothing could be done surgically until Ox directed them in the right direction. Until then, Semaj would have to wait it out and continue to be injected with pain medication.

Only the immediate family was allowed to attend Semaj's burial, and before she was placed into the ground, final words by the preacher would be spoken.

It was a beautiful day despite the obvious. The sun was shining and the birds sang a tune in the trees above. It was like Mother Nature knew that someone was about to become one with her. In the surrounding area, Milano guards stood, armed and patrolling the grounds.

"Are you alright, Uncle?" Marcela asked, seeing that Gio kept grabbing his chest in discomfort.

"Yeah, I'm good, sweetheart. I'm just hurting right now. I'll be fine soon enough," he said, and walked over to the gravesite. The Milano Family all stood around the gravesite and listened to the preacher send Semaj home.

Gio had about enough at this point, and he was no longer able to hold his emotions back as he stood over the casket that was being lowered down into the ground. It was his granddaughter he was burying, and it felt just as bad, if not worse than burying Kasey. One tear led to another, and before anybody knew it he was weeping uncontrollably and calling out Semaj's name.

All eyes turned to look at him. This was the first time he ever cried in front of anybody, so to see it was like seeing the unthinkable.

"My precious baby!" he cried out, wiping the tears from his face with his handkerchief. "I'm sorry, princess!" he continued, falling to his knees.

Sosa quickly ran over to Gio and helped him up. Even though it was only immediate family there, it still wasn't appropriate for the leader of the family to be seen on his knees and crying. He was supposed to be the strongest out of all of them, and now some people were starting to look at him in a different light.

Once off the ground, he looked around at everyone, who was staring right back at him. Before he could say a word and before he could explain his actions, a bullet crashed through his chest and exited his back. A second bullet hit him in his chest again, and as he was falling to the ground, another bullet hit him in the top of his head.

This shocked the hell out of everyone who was looking at him because nobody heard the actual shots. They watched him as he fell into the grave, right on top of Semaj's casket. More bullets continued to spray down on the crowd, causing everyone to scatter. Sosa pulled her Glock .40 from her waist, and looked around to see where the shots were coming from. Marcel and LuLu followed suit, pulling their weapons out in an attempt to get at the shooter.

"Find cover! Everybody, find cover!" Marcel screamed, pushing her family members out of the way.

"Look in the trees!" LuLu yelled, looking up as a flock of birds flew off in a panic.

It was pandemonium in the graveyard, and everybody

was a target. Bullets knocked chunks of marble and stone off the nearby tombstones and kicked up dirt beneath the family's feet as they tried to run for cover.

Carlos, Semaj's first cousin, was hit in his neck when he tried to get up and run towards the cars. Bonjo ran over to him and dragged him behind a large headstone, taking his shirt off and wrapping it around his neck to stop the bleeding.

"I don't see shit!" LuLu yelled out, barely being missed by bullets flying over her head.

Sosa stuck her head from around the tombstone she was taking cover behind and took in a good look around the graveyard. All the screaming and yelling from the people around her had become silent. She could hear herself breathe as her heart tried its best to jump out of her shirt. She gazed up into the trees, but didn't see anything. She observed all the cars and didn't see anything. She looked around at other plots and didn't see anything… that is until she saw a figure sitting behind a Mother Teresa statue at the far end of the yard. The flash from the gun solidified the gunman's location, prompting Sosa to react. "The statue! Behind the statue!" she yelled out to LuLu, who was behind another tombstone.

Emilia had jumped into the grave to help Gio, but when she got there she couldn't believe her eyes. It was too late. Even if he did have on a vest, the head shot was enough by itself to kill him. She just sat there in the grave looking down at Gio, and laid his body out on top of the casket. Tears filled her eyes, but fury filled her heart more. She cried out of anger, climbed out of the grave, and pulled the High Point C .9mm from her back pocket.

One after another, guards were dropping like flies, but fearlessly, LuLu and Sosa started running towards the shooter, firing rapidly and with accuracy.

"Sorry, Mother Teresa!" Sosa prayed as her bullets hit the statue.

A barrage of bullets tearing up the ground forced the girls off their route, so LuLu had to run behind a tree and Sosa behind a brick wall. The sounds of the bullets stopped, but neither of the girls were willing to come from behind their posts quite yet.

Sosa peered around the wall, and what she saw almost took the life out of her. Her jaw dropped to the ground, and for a moment she was stuck in a daze. She was looking at him, and he was staring right back at her. The thick, brown, dread headed man before her very eyes was Ox. It had been like forever since she last saw him, but she knew beyond a shadow of a doubt that it was him. He looked at her and smiled before firing several more shots at her, and then at LuLu behind the tree.

Hatred was the only thing that brought Sosa from behind that wall, and when she came out, she came out firing with everything she had. LuLu, seeing her sister coming out blazing, came out too, doing the same thing. Bullet after bullet knocked chunks of marble out of the Mother Teresa statue. They both fired until their guns were empty. When the smoke cleared, nobody was behind the statue. Ox had disappeared into the daylight like a magician.

"Who da fuck was it?" Marcel asked, damn near out

of breath from running up the small hill.

Sosa just stood there with a blank look on her face, holding the empty gun by her side. She found it hard to swallow, thinking of the man she hated more than anything in the world. "Ox! It was Ox!" she said out of frustration, and then walked off down the hill.

Chapter 2

Nasah pulled up to the place he was supposed to meet a client, and serve him a brick of cocaine. London's drug trade was starting to pick up for The New York boys who came through and turned the city upside down.

Qua was rising to the top like the boss he was, and trailing right behind him was his right-hand man, Nasah. The only problem was that the work was starting to dry up because Qua hadn't been blessed by the new connect yet.

When Nasah got out of the car, he could see Rizzo standing in the doorway talking on his cell phone. The work was never shown until the money was in Nasah's hand. It wasn't the fact that the client wasn't trustworthy; it was Nasah who didn't trust the client, or anybody else for that matter. He knew firsthand that London niggas were just as grimy as any other niggas in the world.

"Nasah, my man! How's it goin', homie?" Rizzo greeted, opening the door so that he could enter the house. "What's up wit' Qua? I thought he was goin' to be wit' you."

"Nah, Qua's taking care of some business right

now, son. You can holla at me," Nasah said while looking around the house.

Turning to look towards the back of the house, he saw two bodies emerge from the kitchen. The two men wore black suits, but didn't flash a badge, which indicated to him that they weren't the police. He quickly pulled his gun from his waist and pointed it at the men. The sound of the hammer cocking back and the feel of the barrel of a revolver being placed to the back of his head made the tension in the room high.

"Oh, yeah, Rizzo?" Nasah said, shocked that he would go that far.

"You must be Nasah," Sidney said, unbuttoning the top button on his suit jacket. "I heard a lot about you. I heard you been in London for a minute now doin' ya thing."

"Yeah, so what's that gotta do wit' you, son?" Nasah shot back while gripping the gun he had in his hand even tighter.

"Look, son, B, or whatever other stupid names y'all call each other in New York, you're in my country now. Fuck, you're in my city! So, here's what's gonna go down, and what I say isn't up for debate. You and ya homie... Qua, is gonna finish up ya business here in London. Then you guys are going to catch the next flight out of here, never to return again."

"You got us fucked up, big man. This is our shit now," Nasah interrupted. "Now maybe if y'all mufuckas stay out the way I could let y'all eat a lil' bit. But just to make this shit clear for you to understand, we ain't goin' a mufuckin' place... *Son!"* Nasah arrogantly said.

Sidney chucked, not because it was funny, but because he was getting irritated already by Nasah's whole demeanor, and the fact that he still had the gun pointed at his face. He had dealt with men coming from all over the world trying to get a piece of London's drug market, but he never came in contact with a nigga like Qua, who had men holding him down to the point where they would take a bullet for him, or may even dispense a few of their own for the cause.

"You heard what I told you," he reminded Nasah as he started to walk past him. The two men held stares for a while before Sidney gave Rizzo the okay to lower his weapon.

Nasah didn't bother to lower his, but rather backed out of the way so that he could put Rizzo in front of his gun. He didn't know how they did it over here in London, but in Brooklyn, shit was done differently. Once you pull a gun out on somebody, you better use it. This wasn't some old mob movie where you make a bunch of threats to a nigga and then turn ya back on him. This wasn't an act where the director yells, "Cut!" This shit was real life.

As the two men walked to the door, Nasah did exactly what any Brooklyn nigga would do. He squeezed off. He spun and hit Rizzo first, because he was the only one who had his gun out. The bullet hit him in his temple, knocking him across the room.

Sidney reached for his pistol but was way too late by the time he got it out. Nasah was already walking up on the two men and firing repeatedly at their upper bodies, striking them both from the neck up. Sidney's body fell out of the front door, while his man dropped in the living room. Nasah just stepped over the bodies like it was nothing, jumped into his car and pulled off.

"I've got another shell casing over here!" Detective Cannon yelled as he walked up the hill at the cemetery.

"We've got a couple more over here!" a detective in another area yelled.

It was like Easter, and the police were hunting for bullets, shell casings, and any other evidence they could find instead of Easter eggs. There were police scattered throughout the entire cemetery.

Some of the officers were questioning the workers who were lowering Semaj's casket into the ground. They also questioned the preacher, who, of course, didn't know much, except that he had done a last minute funeral that paid in cash. He didn't know who he was burying or the name of the person that paid him.

"We've got a lot of blood in here," an officer said, looking into the ground where Semaj's casket was. "Whoever lost this much blood can't be alive," he said to Detective Cannon, who had come and stood next to the grave.

It seemed as if the entire cemetery suddenly got quiet, and every head turned when several large tented SUV's pulled up. A forensics truck followed close behind, and right then and there, Detective Cannon knew exactly who it was. They got out of their vehicles suited and booted.

"FBI!" Agent Flint announced, flashing his badge. "This is now a federal crime scene!" he asserted with a strong tone.

"Says who?" Cannon asked, not moved by his badge. "Last time I looked, we were able to solve cases just as well as you guys, if not better."

"Multi-million dollar drug organization, racketeering, gun smuggling and Mafia ties trump anything you local boys can handle!" Flint shot back.

It was only a matter of time until the feds got involved with the Milano Family. They had drawn enough attention to themselves with all the shootings, bombings, and the large amounts of drugs that was flowing through the city over the past year or so. The investigation officially kicked off and started with Bonjo. He was crazy to think that he was going to walk out of the Federal Building on a bail without cooperating with the government. Letting Bonjo back on the streets was only a part of the government's plan to hit the Milano Family where it was going to hurt.

"We've got an M-16 behind the statue!" an officer yelled out when he discovered the gun.

"Don't touch it!" agent Flint yelled back. He pointed at one of his agents for him to go over there and secure it. "As a matter of fact, if you don't have one of these, I need you to exit the premises," he said, referring to the FBI badge he held in the air.

Flint, like many federal agents, was always leery about the local police when it came down to evidence, especially dealing with the mob. Evidence always seemed to disappear or become misplaced before a trial, just like the body that was missing from inside the grave Flint was looking into. The only reason why it was like that was because of the money that the criminal organization was able to throw around. With the feds, it didn't matter how much money you tried to throw their way, it was to no benefit. The only thing that could help anybody was his or her cooperation. Other than that, a nigga had to be ready to go down with the ship.

Chapter 3

The sounds of a little girl singing rang in Semaj's ears as she lay in the bed. It wasn't the little girl singing that caught her attention though, but what she was singing. It was some sort of Jamaican song, and Semaj knew the accent if she didn't know anything else.

A million thoughts went racing through her mind, and she hadn't even opened her eyes yet. Once she finally did, she found it hard to keep them open because of the bright sun shining through the window. She wanted to say something but she couldn't get the words out of her dry throat. Her eyes began to adjust, and as they did, she saw Qua asleep in a chair next to her bed, and the little girl that was singing was sitting on the floor playing with her toys. Ironically, the little girl was the first person to see her awake.

The little girl walked over to the bed and grabbed a hold of Semaj's hand. "Hi!" she said, with a smile on her face that made the sun seem like it was setting. She was so cute, and the more Semaj looked at her, the more the little girl started to look familiar.

"You got a boo-boo," the girl said, reaching up and

pointing at the bandage wrapped around Semaj's face.

The commotion in the room woke Qua up from his sleep. Seeing Semaj awake was a beautiful start to his day. He immediately walked over to the bed and placed one of her hands into his. "Hey, beautiful!" he spoke gently while caressing the back of her hand.

By now, the little girl took off running into the other room, leaving the two alone.

Semaj still couldn't talk very well, but she had a lot of questions to ask, especially the one about why the little girl was singing a Jamaican song. She looked up at Qua who was looking down at her with a smile on his face. "Where... am... I?" her scratchy throat managed to get out.

"You're safe now. We're in Jamaica—"

"Jamaica!" she shot back, cutting him off in mid-sentence. She almost rolled out of the bed.

"Yeah, we're at my man, Ox's crib. Trust me, you're good, ma," he tried to assure her.

She was trying her best to get out of the bed. Qua could see the fear in her eyes when he said Ox's name. It was like she had seen a ghost, and with all the energy she had she tried to get out of the bed. If she had enough strength, she would have been out the door by now, but the pain medication had her a bit drowsy.

She finally sat up in the bed and looked around the room for her clothes. She saw a gun sitting on the nightstand and quickly grabbed it, and cocked it back slightly to make sure a bullet was in the chamber.

Qua just looked at her like she was crazy, but she

was far from crazy. "Yo, what's wrong with you?" he asked with a concerned look on his face. "Ox is gon' let us know where all this beef you got is coming from."

Semaj didn't say a word. She just continued looking around the room in a panicky manner. She could hear the ocean outside, and at this point she could also hear a couple of Ox's guards outside of the window, apparently kicking a soccer ball around in the open grass.

Qua reached for the gun in Semaj's hand and flinched when she yanked her hand back and took the safety off. He didn't have any idea what he'd just done.

"You telling me you really don't know?" Semaj asked while pointing the gun in Qua's direction in case he was in on it.

"Bay, I don't know what's really good with you, but you're buggin' out right now. I told you, my man Ox—"

"Is he here?" she asked, cutting him off.

"Nah, he didn't get back yet. Just be easy, ma."

"Ox is the one who sent somebody to do this to me!" Semaj said, pointing the gun to her badly burned face. "I'm beefing wit' Ox, Qua! Da nigga's been tryin' to kill me for months now!" Semaj said, looking Qua in his eyes.

Her words smacked him in the face like a bag of bricks, so much so that he flopped back into the chair because his knees started to buckle. Semaj inched her way to the edge of the bed. Her body was aching, and even though she was kind of weak, she managed to get to her feet.

"Exuse me, but I tought ya might wanta know that

Ox'll be 'ere shortly," the maid announced as she stood in the doorway.

Qua jumped up from his chair once the maid left, and ran straight to the balcony to see where the two guards were. He quickly darted across the room and retrieved Semaj's clothes from the closet and tossed them onto the bed right next to her. "I'm getting you da fuck out of here!" he said, feeling stupid that he even brought her into the lion's den. "You have to believe me, ma. I had no idea. I swear, I didn't know!" he repeated, falling to his knees in front of her in an attempt to help her put her pants on. "Damn, I fucked up! I fucked up!"

Sosa sat in Semaj's bedroom, staring out of the open window as the snowflakes fell on her face. She'd been sitting there all night, and the Henny in her glass had all kinds of thoughts racing through her head… Gio getting assassinated, Semaj being murdered, and people in the family starting to fight and bicker. Nothing seemed like it was going right in her life.

She looked off into the sky, and the most important thing she couldn't stop thinking about was her baby… the little girl she never got a chance to hold or feed… the little girl that only became a memory over the past year.

Suddenly, something had hit her. It was like a light bulb turned on in her head after careful thought. The vision of the little Jamaican girl stuck in her head, and it started to eat at her. *Could it be? Could that little girl be mine?*

she wondered, downing another shot of the "devil's juice." She looked to be the right age, and there was something about the little girl's eyes that Sosa couldn't get out of her mind. It was like the little girl was calling out for her.

"What's good wit' you, baby girl?" Marcel asked, entering the room. She had been downstairs with the rest of the family, going over the details for Gio's funeral.

Marcel was the strongest one out of the bunch, and although she was heart stricken about the two most painful loses in her life, she had to maintain some sort of strength for those in the family that couldn't hold it together. She was like everybody's rock.

Sosa could barely talk. The liquor had her completely emotional that she didn't even know what to say, or if anybody would believe her if she told the story of her and Ox's potential child together. She just sat there downing shot after shot until she said, "Fuck it!" and drunk straight from the bottle.

Ox looked out the Lear jet's window as it flew over Jamaica. He was thinking to himself how much pleasure it brought him to put a bullet in Gio's head. The long awaited confrontation paid off in a big way, and the only thing that was stopping him from taking over the East Coast drug trade was Semaj, a person whom he believed to be dead.

It was kind of official that Paris had earned her way

in becoming Ox's chick. She wasn't wifey but she was close to it. She did a hell of a lot of work for him and rode hard with him. It was she who put Ox on to where Semaj's burial site was going to be and she knew that the entire family was going to be there.

"Me wanna t'ank you for 'elpin' me out," Ox said, sitting across from Paris. "If you ride wit' me I gon' make you so rich ya won' be able ta count ya money. I'ma 'bout ta take over the whole East Coast."

Paris didn't want to spoil the day by telling Ox that the person he thought was Semaj really wasn't her. She felt a little bit of fear not knowing how he was going to react to the news. He might think that she was a failure and decide to kill her the minute she got off the plane. He might think she was really riding with the Milano Family, which would make him kill her *before* she got off the plane. All these thoughts ran through her mind as she looked out the small window. Either way, she wasn't saying shit. She just wanted to enjoy the feeling of being someone important to somebody that was important. "So, what are you going to do about the rest of the Milano Family?" she asked out of curiosity while also thinking about the strength the family had.

"Me not gon' do not'in' right now. Once you cut the head off, da body can't function," he said, thinking he was schooling Paris on something she was unfamiliar with. "Right now, the family will grieve, and I will get my money up in the process. If they want to go back to war again, I got a t'ousand bumba-clot soldiers ready to kill for me!" he said, becoming angry at the thought.

"Alright, boo. Don't get ya'self all worked up. The Milano Family is finished, so for you the sky is the limit," she said, and lifted his hand to her lips and kissed it like he was the king of the world.

"No, *mami*, there is no limit to where I'm 'bout to go."

Paris was vicious, but she was playing her cards right. She knew how to do three things very well, and they were: get at a dollar, suck a good dick, and get in where she fit in. Everything she did had a motive behind it, and what she was preparing to do with Ox was far beyond his grasp to comprehend. Right now she wanted to enjoy being in the presence of a boss, and Ox definitely was one of those.

The entire Milano Family sat around the table in the basement of the hospital. Every face was sorrowful and nobody wanted to be there. Nobody even wanted to look at each other, and the only sound in the room came from Sosa's lips sucking on the Henny bottle that she hadn't put down yet. It was a meeting that had to happen in order to establish some important matters.

"Alright, let's get this meeting started," Ortiz said, sitting at the head of the table. "I know that this is a rough time for all of us, but this family needs to keep moving forward if we have any plans on holding it together."

"Holding what together?" LuLu asked with an attitude, not really wanting to hear what Ortiz was talking about.

LuLu was one of the main ones in the room who didn't want to be there. Out of everybody, she took the loss of Gio the hardest. Being honest with herself, she wasn't really that upset about Semaj's death. She felt like all of this shit came about after Gio brought her into the family. She had some love for her, but for her to become the boss within a couple of months of knowing the family business was like a smack in the face. It wasn't that she wanted to run the business herself, but she felt like everything was perfect before Semaj got there.

"The first order of business, which is obvious, is that we need to appoint a new boss to run the family," Ortiz mentioned, looking around the room at the uninterested faces. "I know this is hard, but somebody has got to step up."

"How can you have a meeting so soon? Shit, we didn't even put Gio into the ground yet, and here we go, talking about the next boss!" LuLu interrupted.

Ortiz had about enough of LuLu's outbursts. He was hurting about the loss of Gio too, but he knew what was best for the family. LuLu speaking out the way she did was exactly what was not going to be tolerated. "This is the fucking Mob, LuLu!" he snapped and slammed his hand on the table.

He caught everybody's attention when he did that. He was never known for blowing his cool over anyone, let alone LuLu. "We're not here to be anything other than the Mob. We deal drugs, launder money, gamble illegally. We kill people, and sometimes some of us get killed, but that doesn't mean that we stop being the Mob. We take loses, and then we get over it. That's what we do. We don't show signs of weakness at all. Do you understand me?" he yelled, establishing his dominance over the room.

Sosa just smiled at Ortiz putting LuLu in her place as she took another swig of the bottle. Nobody was really taking the meeting seriously, and Ortiz thought this might not have been a good time to have it. "Now, as I was saying, Bonjo would be the next to step up and run the family, unless someone has a different opinion," he said, trying to get the meeting over with.

No one in the room was crazy enough to say anything about Bonjo, even if they didn't feel like he was the best candidate for the job. He was still crazy and the last person whose bad side you would want to be on. It was a no-brainer, so there were pretty much no objections.

The slums of Jamaica weren't comparable to anything Semaj had ever seen. She been to the beaches of Kingston where tourists go, but the 'hood was totally different. Now she knew why, when she did vacation there, hotel staff told her not to go into the 'hood because she might not make it out. That's just the way she was feeling, walking past shack after shack, abandoned car after abandon car. There were stray dogs lurking about that looked like they hadn't eaten in a few months. The smell of curry in the air was probably the most pleasant thing about the 'hood.

Qua didn't know the first thing about Ox's 'hood,

except for a whorehouse he was brought to once before, but he had to get Semaj out of the house before Ox's plane landed. The jet that he was on was the same one that Qua needed to use to get Semaj out of Jamaica.

It seemed like everybody they passed was stalking them like prey. Semaj held on tightly to the .40 caliber she had under the sheet she had wrapped around her. It seemed to take forever but they finally made it to the whorehouse in the middle of the town.

Michelle met Qua at the door with a smile, remembering him as her "American big spender." But seeing Semaj with a bandage around her face was what quickly grabbed her attention. Qua didn't say a word and really didn't have to once he pulled out a wad of American money.

Michelle looked out the door, up and down the street to see if the wolves had fallen back, which they did. "Come. Me got one last room for ya," she said, and guided them to the second floor of the house.

This wasn't a place where Qua was going to keep Semaj at for long, even though Michelle wasn't a big fan of Ox, who never paid when he come through, tricking. As soon as Qua got the chance, he was out. The one issue he had to debate on was whether or not to kill Ox for trying to kill his girl. The only problem with that was he knew beyond a shadow of a doubt that he wouldn't make it out of Jamaica alive if he did kill him… neither him *or* Semaj.

Chapter 4

Music blasted through the speakers at Club Low where Nasah sat in VIP. Bottles were everywhere, and he was surrounded by a couple of his boys, along with a few chicks. He was having the time of his life since Qua wasn't in town, nor answering his phone.

The coke had dried up, minus what was on the streets at that time. It gotten to the point where Nasah didn't know if Qua was dead or alive. He was even thinking about finding another connect—not permanently but temporarily—until Qua got back to the city with the new work.

The club was jammed packed, wall to wall, and door to door. Through the crowd of dancers, three men in tailored suits made their way over to the VIP section where Nasah was. One was Jeramie, the second son of Ingrid and the brother of Pelpa from the Abbot Family. He was the problem child of the family, and up until his mother's death, he was pretty much tame. He wasn't big on the drug business his family was into. He was more into violence and putting the fear of God into man. It was odd, but that's how he got his kicks. He was the type that would take on the bully in the building, and right now the bully in the building was Nasah. Next to him was his security, as if he ever needed it. It seemed like everybody who was dancing on the floor got out of their way as they passed through.

Jeramie walked right up to the booth and stood in front of the table, already having pulled his gun from his waist when he walked across the room.

The club continued to party as though nothing was going on. People were looking out of the corner of their eyes, knowing that any time Jeramie came around, it was for a reason, and his actions were unpredictable. A couple of females sitting at the table with Nasah had got up, wanting to avoid anything that didn't concern them.

Here we go again! Nasah thought to himself as he reached under the table for the gun he had in his lap. Two of his boys stood by the table, both who acted as if they were going to reach for their guns. "We got guns too, son!" Nasah yelled over the music with a smirk on his face.

Jeramie looked around and saw Nasah. This was the kind of shit he lived for and without a second thought he raised his gun and fired off a shot, hitting Nasah in the chest. Nasah also got off a shot under the table, striking Jeramie in his upper thigh just two inches from his balls.

Jeramie was a like an oak tree. He didn't even budge when the bullet hit him. He squeezed off several more shots before Nasah could get a chance to fire another bullet. His body looked like it was doing the Harlem Shake as six rapidly fired bullets blasted into his body.

The remaining people sitting at the table scattered from the booth. The odd thing about it was that the club continued to party like nothing ever happened. It was either they didn't notice what was going on, or the people who did know what was going on were too scared to move. The music continued to blast through the speakers, and the people continued to dance on the floor.

Nasah's two boys had second thoughts about grabbing the guns they were reaching for after seeing that Jeramie's goons had them on the jump. Putting their hands in the air was probably the only thing that saved their lives.

Jeramie was only there for Nasah and nobody else. He wanted to make an example out of him to let everybody know that these were *his* streets, and anybody that came from the other side of the map trying to take over would pay the ultimate price.

There was nobody else in his family that could tame him, and frankly nobody wanted too, hoping he would be the city's savior from the American goons who were fucking up their streets and the balance of the drug trade. The death of Ingrid and Pelpa was enough to fuel the never-ending flames of war.

Jeramie turned and walked out of the club with the gun still in his hand. The last thing he had to worry about was somebody ratting on him. Nobody was stupid enough.

Nikolai, from the Russian mob, Valentina from Columbia and Marko Dedaj from the Albania Mafia all sat at a table at an undisclosed location, discussing business as usual. Not all families of the 16 Tent families attended this meeting, and that was mainly because the families were beginning to fall off the face of the Earth. In the drug game, only the strong survive, and if you didn't already have your shit together, then up and coming mobs are going to try you to see if they can take over. That was the power struggle that was defeating the Abbott Family, and possibly the Milano family as well.

Sometimes, the meetings didn't start right away for the bosses. They normally sat around and talked big money shit to each other for a while, often debating about who was the richest and what kind of new toys they had brought. There weren't too many people in the world that could match dollar for dollar with Valentina. Her money was literally peaking over a billion, and that was in U.S. currency alone. The only thing she ever talked about at the table was buying more land. Sometimes she made jokes about wanting to buy a section of the Atlantic Ocean, because that was probably the only thing she hadn't purchased yet. Some people took it as a joke, but in all seriousness she wasn't playing around.

Dedaj always talked about his aquarium and the new fish that he added to his collection. He wasn't anywhere near a billion, but he definitely ranked high in the millionaires' club. He had a thing with eating fresh clams, and most of the time he would bring pounds of them to the meetings. Nobody ever wanted to eat them with him though, because of the way they smelled.

"So, it looks as though Europe is open for the taking," Valentina said, starting the meeting off. "It seems like the Abbott Family couldn't hold their ground."

Before Valentina could get out another word, the sound of a cell phone ringing pierced through the room. Everybody got quiet and looked around at each other, wondering where the ringing was coming from. To bosses like the ones in the room, it was like a joke for one of them to have a cell phone. For a boss, there really was no reason for them to carry one. They had people who did stuff like answer phones for them, and whoever did get caught talking on the phone wouldn't hear the last of the jokes, especially the ones that would come from Dedaj.

Today, the culprit was Valentina, the richest person at the table. She was hesitant in answering it because Dedaj had already had a smile from ear to ear on his face, and was already starting to giggle from the anticipation of seeing who was going to pull the phone out. Valentina reached in her Louis Vuitton bag and grabbed the device, giving Dedaj a look like he better not crack nary a joke. "What? It's for family emergencies," Valentina stated and shrugged her shoulders with a guilty grin on her face.

She looked around the room at everybody before they all busted out with snickers and laughs at the "Queen" sticking her earpiece in her ear. "So, you're telling me that nobody in this room has a phone?" she asked before answering hers.

Dedaj was about to answer the question with something slick, but Valentina stopped him, motioning with her index finger to give her a moment.

The voice on the other end of the phone was Semaj, unexpected but welcomed. Her voice sounded weak and broken, and from that Valentina knew that something was wrong. She had to get up from the table in order to hear her, because Dedaj had the rest of the bosses laughing out of control at some of his cell phone jokes.

"Ms. Valentina, I need your help," Semaj said into the phone, trying not to sound weak in what she was asking.

"Anything!" she responded, concerned about her wellbeing.

"I'm stuck in Jamaica and I need a way out. I can't explain everything right now, but if you could send somebody to come get me, I would be indebted to you," she said as she tried to block out the sounds of a Jamaican hooker getting pounded out in the room next door to hers.

"Just get to the beachfront. There's a restaurant

called Diablo's next to the hotels by the main airport. Get there, and tell Rosa, the manager, your name. You should be fine," Valentina assured before Semaj hung up the phone.

Valentina went back to the table and was about to continue the meeting, but again she was interrupted. This time it was Tina, head of security for the 16 Tent meetings, coming into the room and placing her cell phone on the table. She had just gotten off the phone with her people from New York.

"Giorgio Milano was killed yesterday at his granddaughter's funeral. Semaj Milano was also murdered on New Year's Eve. They say it was the Jamaicans," the woman said with a serious look on her face.

Everyone in the room was speechless. Nobody would have ever thought that Gio would go out like that. He had too much pull; too much respect in New York. He was one of Santo Domingo's top three families, and the loss of him was like minority communities losing Barak Obama.

"That's why I don't want a cell phone," Dedaj said, shaking his head and sitting back in his chair with the same blank look that everybody else had on their faces.

Valentina immediately got up from the table and adjourned the meeting, thinking about Semaj and her being trapped inside enemy territory. She was probably the only one who knew Semaj was still alive, where everyone else thought she was dead. Until she figured out what was going on, it would have to stay that way.

"Ox, what's good, old boy?" Qua greeted, meeting him at the front entrance.

Qua didn't notice Paris until she got out of the Range Rover and fixed her clothes. He wondered how in the hell was she here with Ox. *This bitch gets around!* He thought to himself as he watched her get her things out of the truck. He had only met her a couple times back in the States, but she definitely was aware of the relationship he and Semaj had, and knew that if she started running her mouth, it could be a means to an end for not only him, but for Semaj too. He started thinking about the only gun that he had, which Semaj had in the whorehouse, and he quickly came to his senses that his mouthpiece was the only thing that could save him at this point.

"Quasim! Damn, playboy! What you doin' all the way out here?" Paris asked, knowing who he was off the break.

He tried to fake like he didn't know who she was, and gave her a limited acknowledgement with just a peace sign. He wanted to keep their conversation to a minimum, but Paris persisted.

"I heard old girl that killed ya pops got what she deserved last week. You know what they say, what goes around comes right back around on that ass!" She smiled, passing by him with her bags.

Paris made a nigga want to snap her neck and throw

her off the bridge for the way she said shit. She had a nasty mouth, and it was as though everything that came out of it was negative. He brushed off what she had said with a smile and a tilt of his hat, but on the inside he had in his mind that eventually he was going to end up killing her.

"So, what brings you out 'ere?" Ox asked, snapping Qua out of his daze. "My bad for not callin' you back, but I was busy," he said, walking around to the side of the house so they could talk in private.

"Man, I wanted you to know that I got an idea of who killed ya boy," he said, referring to Rude-Boy. "If everything works out, I should have the nigga's head on a silver platter for you by the end of the week," he told Ox, thinking fast on his feet with a good excuse for why he was in Jamaica.

"Yo, that's luv, my nigga! Me gon' take care of you for that. That's me word."

If Ox only knew that he was standing right in front of the man who killed his son, he would have chopped Qua's head clean off of his shoulders without thinking twice.

"I don't mean to sound ungrateful, but tell me one t'ing. I know you didn't come all the way 'ere to tell me that," Ox said with a suspicious eye. "And didn't you say that you had company?" he asked as he looked around the compound.

"Nah, I had the bitch wit' me last night from the whorehouse you put me on. She rolled out this morning though. The other reason why I'm here is because I need you. I needed to get some work from you until my connect comes through. Shit's starting to dry up in the UK, and I just need enough to last me for the rest of the month," Qua said, once again thinking fast on his feet.

"Don't worry. Me gon' put you on da jet wit' many bricks. I gon' get you right. Soon you might not have ta worry about a new connect. I got something big goin' down, and when it comes to me, I gon' bless ya."

Qua was only trying to hold a good enough conversation to make it off the compound. What he said was good enough to convince Ox that there wasn't anything fishy going on. The two men turned to go into the house, and as they were doing so Qua looked out towards the city where Semaj was waiting for him.

Semaj did exactly what Valentina told her to do. The madam of the whorehouse got her a ride to the restaurant that she was supposed to go to, and a woman named Rosa was there waiting to escort her to the airport where she would board a flight to the United States, and then another flight to El Dorado International Airport.

Semaj was given strict instructions to go straight to Valentina without going anyplace else, and that's what she did, even though the layover was in Philadelphia, a mere two and a half hours away from her home in New York.

She had to call Qua to let him know where she was before he got worried. When she dialed his number, he picked up on the second ring. "Qua, it's me," she said, looking out the window at the Philadelphia airport.

Worried to death was an understatement. He had been back to the whorehouse looking for her, and when the madam said that she had left, he didn't know what to think. All Semaj left behind was the gun, and money was the only thing that got the madam to say where the ride took her. Hearing her voice eased his heart and mind. "Damn, ma! Me and you gonna fight!" he joked after she told him where she was. "You must be tryin' to give a nigga a heart attack!"

"I'm sorry. I had to get the hell out of there ASAP."

"Yeah, I was making that happen, ma. I just needed a little more time," he tried to plead, hoping that she understood that he had been doing everything within his power to get her out of there.

"Don't worry, boo. I'll give you an 'A' for effort," she said, trying to make a joke out of the situation.

"Yeah, you got jokes, huh? So now what? When am I gonna see you again?"

"I'm still ya connect, right? Call me when you're ready to re-up. I love you. I got to go. I can't miss this flight," she said when she heard the boarding call for her flight.

"No, no! My name is Samantha Milano!" Sosa yelled into the phone. "Put somebody on the phone that can speak English!" She had been on the phone all day long calling Jamaica, trying to find the doctor that delivered her baby. She wasn't getting anywhere calling from across the water and the frustration was becoming unbearable as she kept getting transferred from office to office.

Sosa came to the realization of what she had to do. She wasn't going to get any answers on the path she was on. The only way she was going to get some clarification was if she took the trip to Jamaica herself. Sosa was certain she could get more answers in person, whether it be voluntarily or by force. No matter which way she went, nothing was going to hold her back from finding out the truth. But before she did anything, she had to get ready to put Gio in the ground.

Chapter 5

Marcela flagged her guards off as she walked into the bodega to serve Cruz two bricks of raw uncut cocaine. Right now, the entire family had to pull together and help keep the daily operations going before people started thinking that the Milano Family was getting sweet. Besides that, there was still a lot of money to be made, and despite the death of an icon, they had to keep moving forward.

Cruz sat behind the counter and waited for the rest of the customers to finish purchasing their items so that he could lock the door and conduct his business. Marcela played it off like she was looking for a pop in the freezer, but what she didn't notice was the wolf standing in the back of the store, lurking and waiting for the opportunity to strike. He quietly walked up behind her and shoved a Glock .9mm into her side in one swift motion. She could feel his heavy breathing on her neck, and in the reflection of the freezer's glass door she could see a distorted image of his face.

Cruz was so busy trying to get the kids from stealing chips from the rack that he didn't even notice what was going on in the back of the store.

"You must be a fuckin' fool to be tryna rob me!" Marcela said, trying to get a better look at him through the glass. "You know who I am?"

The man didn't say a word, but rather stuffed the gun deeper into her ribs. He calmly removed the bag with the two bricks of cocaine in it from off of her shoulder, and gave her one firm warning that if she moved or did anything stupid she was going to be the first person he killed. He slowly reached around her waist and grabbed the gun she had in her waistband. There was no doubt in his mind she was packing. He probably knew more about her than she thought, which put her in the fucked up predicament she was in.

Finally picking his head up from the counter, Cruz was shocked to see the scruffy, old looking man holding Marcela at gunpoint. He reached under the counter for his pistol.

The robber saw his every move and was anticipating him doing that. With the bag draped over his shoulder and Marcela's gun in his pocket, he grabbed a handful of Marcela's hair, turned her around and used her as a human shield.

Cruz didn't want to take the chance of firing while he held her in front of him, but at the same time he wasn't trying to let the man walk out of his store with Marcela or the coke. "Put da mafuckin' gun down!" Cruz yelled out as the robber started walking towards him with Marcela in front of him. "I'm not gonna tell you again, nigga!"

Cruz was about ready to shoot the both of them now, to safeguard the forty thousand he had behind the counter for the score. "Fuck it!" he said and took a potshot in the robber's direction, hitting the potato chip rack right next to Marcela.

The robber returned fire at Cruz while backpedaling and still holding Marcela by the hair. Two bullets hit Cruz; one in the stomach and another in his right shoulder. He dropped to the floor holding his shoulder, because it was the wound that hurt the most.

The two guards heard the shots in the store and came in with their weapons drawn. They quickly eased up at the sight of the man dragging Marcela towards a room that led to the back door. They couldn't get a good look at his face because he had it hidden behind Marcela's head. The two guards followed them cautiously with their guns aimed and ready to shoot at the first good opportunity that presented itself. The robber kicked the back door open, still dragging Marcela with him.

"They are going to kill you, stupid!" she assured the robber. "They won't let you get away!"

Once outside, the robber slammed the door behind them, turned Marcela around and head-butted her before she could get a chance to see his face. The blow knocked her out cold. The perpetrator stood over her, pointed the gun to her head and right when he was about to pull the trigger, gunshots coming from inside of the store forced him to spin away from the back door that had bullets piercing through it. He was going to reposition himself to get the shot off into Marcela's head, but by the time he did, one of the guards had pushed his way out of the back. The gunmen backpedaled down the alleyway, squeezing off shots until the guards could no longer see him.

Gio's funeral was so small that nobody even knew about it but a handful of people. Bonjo was the one who picked his body up and took it away before the cops got to the cemetery. He wouldn't give anyone the pleasure of handling a Mafia boss's body, even if that meant him jumping into Semaj's grave and getting it himself.

Gio's body lay in a white oak casket, with rose gold trimming and 24 carat solid gold handles. He wore an all white Armani suit and a pair of albino rattlesnake skin loafers, and had an all black Audemars Piguet watch around his wrist. It was an open casket funeral. The mortician who took care of his body covered the bullet wound to his head with a small cotton pillow that fitted in the casket.

Ortiz, LuLu, Sosa, Marcela, JahJah, Emilia and Bonjo sat in the little room, grieving his death. Emilia couldn't bear to look at him, or even stay in the same room as the tears rolling off her face were the least sign of the pain she was suffering.

LuLu was hurting, but not as much as everybody else. She never forgot Gio threatening to send her back to Santo Domingo for the situation that happened with Semaj. But for the most part, there wasn't a dry eye in the room as everybody took his death hard.

The sound of a door opening and closing at the front of the funeral home caught everybody's attention, and LuLu and Sosa instantly stood up and pulled out their weapons. Everyone else in the room followed suit, and pointed their weapons at the front door.

The very moment the double doors to the room opened, safeties came off the weapons, and they were itching to get to blasting. To everyone's disappointment, a single person came through the door. The woman pulled her hood back revealing herself to the family, and to their surprise, Semaj was standing before them.

Sosa became so weak at the knees she almost fell over. She was the first one to run over to her. She wrapped her arms around her waist and gave Semaj a heartfelt embrace.

"Maj?" Emilia asked, still confused as to whether or not this was really her. JahJah couldn't hold the contents in her stomach. She threw up in between the pews.

Ortiz walked up to her and kissed her on the forehead, smiling at the sight of his niece, the princess. Bonjo embraced her as well, along with Marcela and Emilia.

LuLu stood off in the back, not really intrigued by her entrance. LuLu had anger and animosity built up for Semaj that reached way beyond her being alive. Deep down inside, she was somewhat glad when it was believed Semaj was dead but in a matter of seconds that had all changed.

Semaj walked up to the casket and looked down at

her grandfather in disbelief. *How did this shit get so out of hand? If the game can bury you then none of us are exempt.* she thought to herself as she gently put her hand on top of his.

Besides the fact that Gio was laid out in a coffin, Semaj felt a negative energy in the room. She looked around and spotted LuLu standing in the back corner giving her a glare that signified hatred. It was a look she'd never gotten from LuLu before, but always felt was there. "What, I can't get no love?" Semaj asked her, breaking the stare between the two.

"Love? All this shit is your fault anyway!" LuLu spat back in an aggressive tone.

"Whoa, whoa, whoa, LuLu!" Bonjo said, coming across the room to check her.

"Shit, it is!" LuLu continued. "Ever since she came into our family, shit's been going downhill. Bringing in these sneaky, conniving niggas like Vega fucked up the natural flow of things. Paulie, great-grand-pop, Uncle Gio… fuck! You even got your own damn father killed behind ya bullshit!"

Semaj just stood there with her hands in her pockets, taking in everything LuLu was saying. Some of the things she was saying were hitting home, especially when she mentioned Murda Mitch, her father.

It was all starting to come to the surface. LuLu had these feelings built up inside of her for a long time. From the beginning LuLu didn't want Semaj running the family business. She always felt like one of the Milano Hitters should be at the helm.

"LuLu, you need to calm da fuck down before you say some shit you can't take back!" Sosa interjected.

"I ain't gotta do shit!" she shot back. "You ain't no fuckin' leader! The only place you're gon' lead us is six feet under just like ya fuckin' son!"

Semaj didn't give her the chance to speak another word. She pulled the chrome .40 caliber from out of her jacket pocket and pointed it right at LuLu's head.

Reacting automatically, Marcel pointed her gun at Semaj's head from the side, instantly protecting her sister first.

LuLu looked in astonishment at the gun pointed at her face, but by no means was she afraid. She actually liked the rush it was giving her, looking death in the face. "Shoot! Pull the fuckin trigger!" she encouraged Semaj taking a step closer. "Yeah, I see you're still shy on the trigger!" she teased.

LuLu didn't realize that Semaj had changed. She wasn't the same person she was a couple of weeks ago, nor was her homicide game lacking in any aspect. LuLu was pushing the right buttons if she was trying to find herself lying in a casket next to Gio.

"Semaj!" Ortiz yelled, walking up and getting in between the gun and Semaj. "You're disrespecting your grandfather at his funeral…all of you!" he yelled, looking around the room.

Marcela slowly lowered her weapon, coming to her senses as she looked at what was transpiring.

LuLu and Semaj held their stares for a while, until Semaj looked over at her grandfather lying in the casket.

She too felt a sense of guilt, and slowly lowered her weapon.

The one thing that Sosa said was more than the truth. LuLu had said something that she wasn't going to be able to take back, nor make up for it. She had gone too far.

"This is what the family has turned into after I supposedly died?" Semaj said, throwing Ortiz a sharp look that cut through his heart. "I'm done, Uncle! You can run this family the way you want!" she said, before turning to kiss her grandfather before she left.

Chapter 6

"If I Was A Rich Girl" banged through the speakers at Ox's club. He sat in the executive section, blowing on some of the sickest weed grown in Jamaica. Paris was sitting next to him sipping on a bottle of Ace and enjoying the view of the strippers dipping it low to the ground, and then popping it back up.

Party lights flashed on and off as the disco ball twirled on the middle of the ceiling. There was ass jiggling all over the place, and there were so many single dollar bills in the place that you could reach down to the floor and pay for your drink when you wanted to.

"Me gon' set you up in London wit' my man," Ox told Paris before he took in a deep drag of the weed.

This caught Paris off guard, but she was well aware of what he was suggesting. She had to nip that in the bud before it manifested into reality. It was bad enough being far away out in Jamaica with Ox, but there was no way in hell she wanted him to ship her ass to London. Home sickness was already starting to set in, and she wanted nothing more than to be back in New York. "That's not going to work, Ox," she said, putting the bottle down and turning to face him.

"Why you t'ink dat?" he asked, looking off into the club.

"I don't know if you knew this or not, but Quasim and Semaj were together at one point."

"What do you mean by togeda?" he turned to her and asked.

"Like in a relationship kind of way. I'm not gonna be sitting up in London waiting for him to figure out that I was the one who killed his girl," she informed Ox. "If I was you, I wouldn't be getting too comfortable dealing wit' da nigga either. You know Gio was like a father to him. Word gets out that you…"

Ox backhanded the shit out of Paris before she could get the rest of her sentence out. He then grabbed her by the throat with the same hand.

Paris was earning her way to becoming part of Ox's crew, but it was way too early to be making threats on his life. This was still Ox. "If word gets out, what?" he asked, gripping her neck tighter. "What him gon' do to Ox?" he asked with clenched teeth.

Paris must have lost her got damn mind for a moment. She totally forgot that Jamaicans didn't have any problems beating their women's asses for poppin' off slick at the mouth. She was no different, and she had to be extra careful because she had one of the slickest mouths that ever came out of New York. But for sure, on the flip side of the coin, this ass whooping came with a price; a heavy price that Ox was going to pay for, one way or the other.

He choked her just a little harder before letting her go. He got back to smoking his ganja like nothing ever happened, leaving Paris sitting in the corner looking stupid and trying to catch her breath. He glanced off into the crowd, but she kept her eyes on him for the rest of the night. *I got something for that ass!* she thought to herself as she rubbed at the hand marks on her neck. *I got something good for you, pussy!*

Quasim sat in his office going over the plans he had for Nasah's funeral. He couldn't help but to think about Nasah, and how he felt somewhat responsible for his death. It was Qua that had brought him out to London to get at a dollar, and now by tomorrow morning he was going to bury him.

Nasah's body was sent back to New York for the official funeral. *As soon as the funeral is over, I'ma make it my business to find out who killed my boy,* he thought to himself as he looked out the office window at the cars driving by outside. Nobody was talking and from what Quasim heard, there were over three hundred people in the club that night but all of them seemed to be on mute.

As Quasim was about to get lost in his thoughts, Jeramie walked into the office unannounced, accompanied by two of his henchmen. When Qua turned around in his chair, he knew it had to be the man that he was soon going to end up killing. He could tell by his aura that the man in front of him was the boss type, fitting the description that some of his workers gave him.

"I hope I'm not interrupting you," Jeramie said, walking over to the table and taking a seat in the chair on the opposite side of Qua.

Qua looked at him and scooted his chair closer to the desk and placed his hand on the butt of the 12-guage pump strapped under the desk. He wanted to hug the trigger right then and there, but decided not to before he got a chance to see what the encounter was going to be about. Any wrong moves on Jeramie's part, he was going to be the first person to catch the shotgun blast. "Yeah, you were. What can I do for you, my man?" Qua asked, leaning slightly back in his chair but steadily gripping the pump.

"You can take ya hand off the shotgun. This isn't that kind of visit," Jeramie suggested after noticing Qua's move. "If I wanted to do something to you, I would have done it when you grabbed ya cappuccino this morning from the coffee shop down the street," he said. He then dismissed the two henchmen and ordered them to stand outside.

Having the opportunity of killing him this morning might have been true, and making his guards leave the room was a sign of a good gesture, but there was no way in hell Qua was going to take his hand off the pump. A single man could kill just as well as three. "So, what are you here for? Wait, let me guess. You must be Jeramie," Qua stated, looking Nasah's killer in the eyes.

"That's right," he answered, moving some of Qua's things to the side in order to kick his feet up on his desk.

"I'm not the kind of guy to beat around the bush, so let me get to the point as to why I'm here. Aside from ya club you got here and a couple of properties you've purchased in the past few months, I know that you're running cocaine in my city. You're what they call 'the man' around here."

"So, what's that got to do wit' you?" Qua asked, wanting him to get to the point.

"I figure that me and you can go into business together. If you got the right connections me and you could run this town."

"I already run this town!" Qua shot back.

Jeramie just laughed at the thought of how serious Quasim felt he was. "See, that's where you're wrong. Do you really believe that you could come all the way from New York to another country and take over one of the largest cities in it? You only made it this far because you wasn't making any real money in the past. Now your name is buzzing around here, which make goons like me who really run this city come out to see what all the buzz is about," Jeramie said. His voice started to rise with a hint of anger behind it.

"And what if I don't wanna do business with you? Then what?" Qua asked, gripping the pump just a little tighter.

"In a nutshell, I'ma send you back to New York in a body bag!" he threatened, not at all being scared of the shotgun pointed at him. "It's simple. You can start making millions, or you can make nothing."

Qua could see the sincerity and conviction in

Jeramie's eyes when he spoke. Although he wanted to, he knew that if he pulled the trigger on him, he wouldn't make it out of the building alive.

There was another thing Jeramie said that caught Quasim's attention and had his mind racing. It was the part about making millions. With the club and the few bricks he was buying at a time, Quasim was only making a couple hundred grand a month. That would soon change once Semaj came back into play, but right now, for some reason, he was kind of interested in what Jeramie had planned. It wasn't that he was afraid of him, but the only thing that could ever change a nigga's mind about anything was money. That's why they call it the root of all evil. "Millions, huh?" Qua said, loosening his grip on the pump.

"Yeah, millions."

"So, what you had in mind" Qua asked, leaning forward in his chair.

"You ever hear of the 16 Tent?"

Sosa boarded the flight to Jamaica with one thing on her mind; Nyala. She felt obligated to find out if the little girl was hers. After seeing what Semaj went through over her son's death, it sparked the instinct of motherhood inside of Sosa.

Her visit to Kingston definitely wasn't going to be a friendly one, and all her questions had better be answered correctly. Hell, if the opportunity presented itself, Sosa wouldn't hesitate to finish Ox's ass off too. Hopefully, the blessing of killing two birds with one stone would manifest into reality, but if accomplishing the goal of bringing her daughter home came first and killing Ox had to come at a later time, then that would be fine too. No matter what, Sosa was about to wake Jamaica up.

JahJah pulled up to the family's funeral home after getting a call from one of the workers who told her that the building was on fire. When she got out of the car, she saw that the building was engulfed in flames. People stood around watching and pointing at the fire as it ripped through each section of the funeral home. Smoke was everywhere, and the sounds of the fire truck sirens were off in the far distance. Her initial gut instinct told her this wasn't any accidental fire.

She immediately jumped on the phone to call Ortiz to let him know what was going on. JahJah was so focused on the conversation that she didn't notice the scruffy haired man approaching her when she started to get back into the car. It was the same man that Marcela had encountered in the store. He was using the same gun he was going to kill her with.

When she got into the driver's side, he was opening the passenger door and climbing in with the gun in his hand pointed right at JahJah. She looked over at the man, then at the gun, then back up at him. Ortiz was still on the phone talking, but JahJah wasn't listening. "Do you know who I am?" she asked the man with an arrogant look on her face, hoping that he realized who she might be and decide to abort his mission.

"Yeah, yeah, yeah," the man said. He cocked his arm back and swung the gun at her face. The slide of the husky automatic cracked JahJah in the mouth knocking out three of her front teeth and damn near putting her to sleep. The cell phone dropped, but Ortiz could hear everything that was going on because the phone was still on.

"Hold up! Stop! Wait!" she pleaded as the gunman continued whacking her in the face with the gun.

The smoke from the burning building passed over the car so the bystanders couldn't see what was actually happening in the car. Blood from the blows splattered all over the windshield and driver's side window, and the sounds of Ortiz screaming out JahJah's name through the phone could be heard throughout the car as the beating continued. He had to have hit JahJah over ten times in the face before she finally gave up struggling. She passed out after the final strike to the side of her forehead.

The man tossed the bloody gun on the floor, grabbed JahJah and flipped her into the back seat of the car. He used his sleeve to wipe the blood off of the window, and pulled off right before the fire trucks and police arrived on the scene.

Chapter 7

Semaj leaned over the wooden fence, looking off into a beautiful view of the pasture that surrounded Valentina's compound. The sun was just about to rise and a breeze blew past her. This would probably be the coolest part of the day, because ninety-degree weather was expected when the morning turned into afternoon. It was so peaceful, and Semaj thought that she could stay there forever. Valentina walked up behind her and broke her concentration, but not enough for her to stop enjoying the scenery.

"It's beautiful, isn't it?" Valentina asked as she leaned up against the fence with her.

"Yes," Semaj replied with a smile on her face. "I could sit out here all day. I can see why you don't leave home much."

"Well, if you work hard enough, maybe one day you can have a pasture of your own to relax in," she advised in her heavy Columbian accent.

"Yeah, well, it looks like I've got a lot of work ahead of me," Semaj said in a sad way.

She had told Valentina about the situation that

happened at the funeral, and how Ortiz pretty much banished her from the family for pulling a gun out on LuLu. It was like being at ground zero, having everything stripped from her in a matter of a few days. *How could I go from being broke as shit to becoming one of the East Coast's most prominent drug suppliers, to becoming broke all over again?* Semaj thought to herself.

I'm not going to lie to you, Ms. Espriella. I don't have anything right now. They took everything. But I promise, when I get back on my feet I'll repay you for allowing me to stay here."

Valentina let out a laugh, grabbed Semaj's arm and pulled her away from the fence to take a walk with her.

Valentina was in her late fifty's but well preserved in her looks. She could easily pass for forty on a bad day. Her deep Columbian roots provided her with long, silky black hair that reached to the top of her butt. Her naturally smooth skin only showed a few wrinkles in a couple spots, and her energy level at times was that of a woman in her twenties.

"I don't have a problem with you staying here, but I'm not a woman that gives handouts. You've gotta earn your living around here just like everybody else."

"Oh, I have no problem with that. Just let me know what you need me to do and it's done." Semaj was under the impression that Valentina was going to have her doing something that she was familiar with, like selling drugs for her or transporting drugs across the border. Any position in one of Columbia's largest drug cartels would be better than what she had.

But it was Valentina who had other plans for the pretty, scar faced threat, and what she had in store was beyond Semaj's comprehension.

JahJah woke up. The man that beat her half to death was squatting over her with a gun in his hand. She could hardly see out of either of her eyes because they were swollen shut for the most part. Blood covered her face and stained her clothes, and she often had to spit out the blood that kept building up in her mouth from where the missing teeth use to be. She still didn't know who the guy was that did this to her, and she wished he'd just kill her and get it over with.

"How much do you think you're worth?" the man asked. He sounded like he had permanent phlegm stuck in his throat.

When she didn't answer, he repeated the question again, this time flipping out JahJah's cell phone. He started scrolling through the memory until he got to Bonjo's name. He then pressed the talk button.

Bonjo picked up on the first ring. He had been anticipating the call. The man didn't say a word but rather put the phone to JahJah's face so that she could talk.

"Hello!" Bonjo yelled into the phone after not hearing anybody on the other end. "Yo-o-o!" he yelled again.

"I want a million for your release," he told JahJah to inform him.

"Jo," a weak raspy voice spoke into the phone getting Bonjo's full attention. "He said he wants a million or he's gonna kill me," she said before coughing and spitting out blood.

"Alright, baby, I got you!" Bonjo assured her. "Just give whoever got you the phone." Hearing her voice sent chills down his spine. JahJah was his baby. She was probably the only woman he loved outside of his family. He would have given five million to whoever it was if they had asked for it.

"Bring the money to the middle of the Brooklyn Bridge in two hours," the man said, and then hung up the phone.

He then took the cell phone and broke it in half with his bare hands and tossed it across the room. There would be no callbacks, no negotiations, and no pleading for her. The money had better be on the Brooklyn Bridge in two hours, not a minute before or a minute after. It was imperative that Bonjo didn't play any games. JahJah's life was depending on it.

Semaj found herself in the middle of a coca field on all fours, picking plants and spraying insecticide everywhere. This definitely wasn't what she had in mind when she agreed to earn her keep. She had dirt all over her clothes, and the ninety-degree weather was taking a toll on her skin. The large flower hat only provided shade for her face, which she needed the most because of her scar.

Valentina wasn't having any mercy on Semaj, not even considering her injury. She was now the help, just like all the rest of the workers that sweated and slaved to make a living. "You look tired, and it ain't even one yet," Valentina said, walking up with a beach chair and taking a seat in the section where Semaj was working. The field was so large that it took a golf cart ten minutes to bring her to where Semaj was working. She too had on a straw hat, but also a bottle of ice-cold lemonade. You could see the frost chilling the bottle, and not even a drop was offered to Semaj.

Damn! She could at least offer me something to drink! Semaj thought to herself as she continued pulling plants out and putting them into the bin next to her.

Just when she thought Valentina was going to be generous and share, she walked over, picked a leaf from off of one of the plants and passed it to her. Semaj looked at her like she was crazy. What's this for?" she asked Valentina with a confused look on her face.

"Chew on it. It will give you a little energy," Valentina advised, and walked back over to her chair.

Semaj looked at it with disgust. To her it was still coke, and she never did coke a day in her life. She looked up at Valentina, who was drinking the lemonade, and then at the sun blazing down on her. *It couldn't get any worse than this,* she thought, and popped the leaf into her mouth. "How long do I have to be out here?" she asked, and bit down on the leaf.

"Until five. You go back to the compound, take a

shower, eat a meal and then rest. You're going to need it, because by seven in the morning you'll be right back here."

Just the thought of it made Semaj want to get up, pack the little bit of shit she had and leave. She had never worked this hard in her life for the amount of money Valentina was paying her.

For the next couple of hours, Valentina sat in the field and watched Semaj break her back picking and planting new trees. She hardly said a word, but rather just watched as Semaj went from section to section. One thing that was noticeable was that the coca leaf she was chewing on had her moving with ease. Valentina just laughed on the inside, because she knew what it was going to do to her.

Bonjo pulled onto the Brooklyn Bridge in exactly two hours as instructed. He didn't know what he was getting into or where JahJah was going to be. He was headed into this blind, but with Emilia and Marcela at both ends of the bridge, he felt a little safer, not that he was scared.

He pulled directly over to what he felt was the middle of the bridge and opened up his hood like he had car trouble in case the police came by. He didn't know why the kidnapper picked this spot over all the places he could have chosen in New York. Ever since 9/11, the cops frequently walked up and down the bridge throughout the day.

"Where da fuck is he?" Bonjo mumbled out loud as he looked to the side of the bridge where there was a pedestrian walkway.

Ortiz sat in the house, waiting to hear the good news that the ransom was paid and JahJah was on her way home. He just sat on the couch and said a prayer, asking his God to make sure that the transaction was successful. Too many people had died in his family, and he wasn't sure how many more deaths it would take before the family reached its breaking point. Ortiz was sitting there thinking that someone has got it out for them, and how it couldn't be Ox this time, because he wouldn't waste time trying to rob them. *Who da fuck is it? I wish da mufucka would show himself so I can put a bullet in his head.*
"*Click! Clack!*"

The sound of a gun being cocked brought him out of his meditative state. When he turned around, his heart dropped into his stomach when he saw a face he thought he'd never see again. If he never felt the feeling of fear before, now was the moment it entered into his heart. It was Murda Mitch, standing behind the barrel of the P-80 Ruger with nothing but death in his eyes. Ortiz couldn't even get a chance to speak as Mitch tossed him a roll of duct tape.

"Ya mouth!" was the only thing Mitch said to him as

he walked around to the front of the couch.

"Mitch, you don't have to do this, man!" Ortiz pled as he ripped a piece of tape off the roll. "We can talk about it," he continued.

Mitch didn't want to hear anything. That's the reason why he gave Ortiz the tape in the first place.

Ortiz never saw this coming. He thought that Gio had killed Mitch a long time ago. What he didn't know was that Gio stood by his word to keep him healthy, so that he could torture Mitch and give him a brutal death as opposed to a quick one. He did just that, locking Mitch up in a concealed section of the hospital that nobody knew about. Gio continually nursed Mitch back to health, only to torture him again.

This went on for quite some time, until the day Semaj died, or at least when Gio thought she had died. Gio went down to the room and told Mitch that Semaj was dead. He cut Mitch free, right then and there. Mitch was half-dead, broke and full of hatred.

That was the dumbest thing Gio could have done, but to him it was the most sensible. If he couldn't keep Semaj alive, how could he blame Mitch for not keeping Kasey alive? Guilt. That's all it was, and from a father's standpoint, he started to understand how sometimes not even the most notorious killer can beat fate. Now a madman was loose, and he was going to stop at nothing until everyone responsible paid for the death of his daughter.

He grabbed Ortiz by the back of his collar and dragged him upstairs to Gio's old office. He knew exactly where everything was, so Ortiz couldn't lie to him about anything, which he tried to do anyway. He must have forgotten that Mitch used to work for Gio as his number-one henchman, and there weren't too many secrets that Gio hid from him. "Now, open the safe!" Mitch demanded, pushing Ortiz over to the desk.

Ortiz couldn't speak, but he gave Mitch a look like he didn't know what he was talking about.

Mitch walked over to the desk and flipped it over, revealing a floor mat underneath it. He pulled that off too, revealing the door to a large floor safe. It kind of shocked him that the safe was still there. He thought that Gio might have moved it, or that Ortiz might not have known where it was.

Mitch walked over to Ortiz and pointed the gun at his head. That alone didn't scare Ortiz, and with that, Mitch thought about it. "Oh, I forgot, you're a gangsta, huh?" he said, tucking the gun into his back pocket.

He looked around the room for something he could use. He had to improvise. He didn't think that he would have had to go this far with Ortiz, so he didn't bring his torture kit. He laid his eyes on the most common thing in the room, an ink pen. He walked over and retrieved it off of the desk, and walked back over to Ortiz with a creepy smile on his face.

"You see this?" he asked, waving the pen in front of Ortiz's face. "I know it don't look dangerous, but sometimes it's not the tool that matters, it's how you use it," he calmly explained. "Now, if you don't open the safe I'ma shove this pen up ya fuckin' nose until it pierces ya brain. And if it don't pierce ya brain I'm gonna have fun tryin'," Mitch threatened.

Ortiz just looked at him without moving. He acted as if Mitch wouldn't follow through with his threat... that is until Mitch leaned over, grabbed the back of his head and began trying to shove the pen up his nose.

Ortiz wiggled his head and tried his best to scream through the tape. He was a gangsta, but there was only so much a gangsta could take before he broke. "M-m-m-m-m-m-m!" he yelled through the tape while nodding his head yes to imply that he was going to open the safe. He rolled over, got on his knees and crawled over to the safe. He could hardly breathe from all the struggling he did.

Mitch stood over him and watched as he spun the dial from left to right. He turned around and looked at Mitch to let him know that the safe was open. Mitch walked over and pulled the door open. *Jackpot!* he thought to himself when he saw the stacks of money.

At that point, there was no need for Ortiz any more. Mitch stood over him and pointed the gun at his head, looking at the fear in his eyes. This is what he wanted to see from all of his future victims. "Ya'll killed my daughter," he said, pointing the gun a little closer.

Ortiz tried to scream through the tape to tell Mitch that Semaj wasn't dead. Mitch didn't know this, and maybe if he did know she was alive, he might not kill him. But it was too late. Mitch pulled the trigger, sending a bullet through Ortiz's skull.

That was nothing but wishful thinking from Ortiz because he was dead the minute Mitch had set foot in the door, but Mitch only prolonged it when he decided to get something out of it. He bagged up all the money and left, leaving Ortiz in a pool of blood.

Semaj went straight to her room and got right into the bed. She was too tired to even think about eating, and she had to have at least seven coca leaves the entire time she was outside. Valentina had worked her like a Hebrew slave, and just thinking about the fact that she had to get up at seven to start the process all over again made her pass up a shower.

She sat on the edge of the bed, inching her boots off. She lay back on the bed for a moment to stretch out, and before she knew it, she was off to la-la land. She went straight to sleep, and was snoring within a couple minutes.

Valentina made her way up to Semaj's sleeping quarters where she almost busted out laughing at Semaj asleep in full gear. "Old city girl never did any hard work!" she chuckled to herself, walking up and taking a seat next to Semaj on the bed. She took the cream she had brought up for her and applied it to the burn on the side of her face. Semaj didn't even feel it, because she was completely knocked out. Valentina walked out of the room, leaving the cream on the table.

Chapter 8

Everyone Sosa talked to in the hospital was acting stupid, as if they didn't know anything. It got irritating being passed around from person to person in an attempt to find her medical records. This was definitely the hospital, and there were a couple familiar faces in the place that Sosa recognized. They too were acting like they couldn't help her.

She had to be careful though, because she didn't want word getting around that she was in Jamaica. Ox would have a field day with her if he caught her there, especially without the security of her sisters.

The process of getting any answers was more difficult than she thought it would be, so it was time to move on to a new method of trying to get some understanding about the situation at hand. First and foremost, before anything else was to be done, she was going to need a gun. She traveled with plenty of money, so finding one shouldn't be a problem at all.

Sosa made one more walk through the hospital, taking down information that was going to be useful to her. Since they wanted to play games, she was going to play games too, but it was guaranteed that nobody was going to be laughing.

Michelle had Ox's dick in the back of her throat as her head bobbed up and down at a fast pace. She was the best whore in the house, and ranked number one for the best dick sucker in Jamaica. There wasn't a soul on the Island that could last over four minutes with her mouth wrapped around his dick, and that included Ox, the only man that made it to three minutes and forty two seconds, flat.

He grabbed the back of her head as the warm spit dripped down his balls, making it hard for him to control himself. He looked over at the clock, and it had only been three minutes since she started. He wanted to try and break his record tonight. When he tried to lift her head off of him, she latched on to his dick even harder, and her mouth became like a lubricated suction cup, which made it hard for Ox to do what he wanted to do. "Bumba-clot!" he yelled out, having to hold onto the back of her head with both of his hands when he reached his climax.

The nut splashed out of his dick and into the back of Michelle's throat causing yet another exhilarating sensation; the kind that made a nigga's foot catch a cramp from it curling too much.

"Damn, girl! Me gon' haf ta stop fuckin' wit' chu!" Ox joked. "I can't even break my own record!"

"See? And ta t'ink I almost couldn't see you tonight," Michelle said, and rolled over on the bed to grab a stick of weed off of the nightstand.

"What chu mean by dat?" he asked, thinking about what she just said.

"Ya friend came by 'ere wit' some girl. She didn't…"

"What friend you talkin' about?" he shot back, cutting her off.

"Ya friend, Quasim. He had some girl wit' 'im. She look bad too." Michelle laughed, thinking about the bandages wrapped around the girl's face. "I got her a ride to the coastline. I 'eard her talking on da phone about goin' bock to da States."

Ox sat up in the bed and got to thinking real hard. Michelle reached over and grabbed a handful of his dick like she was ready to go for round two, but Ox wasn't in the mood anymore. His mind started wandering off, thinking about all the things that Paris had told him about Qua, and how close he was to Gio and Semaj. For some odd reason, he even started thinking about his son, and how Qua told him how he died in London.

A lot of shit wasn't adding up, and Ox wasn't stupid to any degree, especially when it came down to treachery. He didn't know who the chick he had with him was, but he was sure going to find out. If Qua turned out to be someone different than who he said he was, Ox wasn't going to waste any time treating him the same way he treated his enemies. All that friendship shit was going out the door.

"So, why are we letting him take the boss role again?" Chazz asked Jeramie, looking in his eyes for a good answer.

"Because the Abbott Family is dead, my stepmother is gone, and my brother is dead right along with her."

"Yeah, so that's even better for you, right? It's your time to step up and hold the family name. You're like the last one still alive."

"I am the last one, but the members of the 16 Tent will never let me take a seat at the table, not after everything I've done."

Jeramie was one hundred percent right about the 16 Tent not allowing him in. He wore out his welcome a long time ago, causing somewhat of a war with Nigeria over territory that didn't belong to him or the Abbott Family. That incident alone cost a few million in damages, a countless number of murders, and an entire four months of negotiating to reconcile the two family's problems, Jeramie was shunned by his own family for that. Plus, in the midst of everything, he brought some unnecessary attention from federal authorities.

On top of all that, Jeramie was too aggressive and his temper was uncontrollable. He wasn't a thinker and did shit very sloppily. That was exactly the kind of foolishness that wasn't allowed, and damn sure wasn't tolerated. Him sitting at the table would be like placing cancer into a healthy body.

"It's time to start over, my friend. It's time we start a new family. You will be by Qua's side at the meetings, and you will take part in all the negotiations. Once you get in with the other families and establish your name, there won't be a need for Mr. Quasim anymore."

Qua was his last chance to get inside of the multi-billion dollar drug industry. Placing him in a position to sit in front of the world's biggest distributors was just the same as him being in the Tent meetings himself. Qua was a perfect candidate, being somewhat well established in London in the drug game. He was just going to be a face… a front… and if need be, a fall guy for when shit got ugly. Nothing would ever come back to Jeramie, even though he would be the one pulling all the strings behind the scenes the entire time.

Without Qua, the only thing Jeramie could do at this point was live the rest of his life hustling low-level quantities of coke, and taxing other drug dealers that hustled in his neighborhood; nothing major, just nickel and dime money, something he had already gotten tired of. It was time to start seeing real money; the kind of money that machines had to count out for you.

Bonjo, Marcela, Emelia and LuLu were in Gio's old office, standing around Ortiz's dead body next to an empty safe.

Bonjo couldn't believe he fell for the Brooklyn Bridge move that took him two hours away from the house, leaving Ortiz at home alone and unprotected. The worst part about it all was that JahJah was still out there, probably dead by now, and Sosa's cell phone was off, indicating to Bonjo that she might have gotten snatched up too.

"Those fuckin' Jamaicans gotta go!" LuLu said angrily. "I don't give a fuck if I got to fly to Jamaica and kill Ox myself, this shit's gotta end!"

"How do you know the Jakes did this?" Marcela asked, walking over to put a sheet over Ortiz's body.

"It's gotta be them. They're the only mufackas we're beefin' with. It…"

"It's not the Jamaicans that did this," Bonjo cut in after taking some time to think about everything that transpired. "Jamaicans don't kill like this."

"What you mean by that?" Emilia questioned while walking over from the other side of the room.

"How many people in this room knew that there was a safe in here?" he asked, pointing to the empty safe on the floor. "Nobody, that's who. Whoever did this planned this shit. It was a robbery, not just a murder. That's what Jamaicans do. They just kill shit. They don't think about robbing the person they're after. Ox's people don't kidnap either. Why would they?"

"So, are you sayin' it's somebody else?" LuLu asked him with a confused look on her face.

"Yeah, and I don't have the slightest idea who it is."

"This family is falling apart!" Marcela said, and lowered her head in sorrow.

Hit after hit was what made Marcela tell the truth. It wasn't just anybody getting shot; it was the bosses being put in the dirt like they meant nothing. That just doesn't happen in the Mafia world. Bosses are well protected, and the only way one could be killed is if he was caught slippin', or died from natural causes.

The Milano bosses looked as if they have been slippin' too much as of late, and it wasn't just family members who noticed it. Everybody saw it. Even the wolves and niggas were beginning to think that they were getting soft. It was getting to the point where the money was even becoming funny, and the need to buy more cocaine was evident. The worst thing a nigga could think in New York was that the family was wounded. Once New York wolves smelled blood, they would be coming for it, fangs first.

The sound of a phone ringing snapped everybody out of their dazes. They looked around at each other to see whose phone it was, and shockingly, it was Gio's office phone sitting on his desk.

Bonjo turned around and grabbed the receiver, wondering who the fuck could be calling this line. "Who's calling?" he answered, looking around the room at the blank faces.

"Jo... Im sorry!" JahJah cried into the phone.

"Jah, where are you?" Bonjo yelled, hoping she was let go.

"I'm not gonna stop until I kill every last one of y'all!" a dark voice calmly said into the phone after snatching it from JahJah.

"Ain't no bitch in my blood, homes! If you was a real nigga you would come see me! I'll meet you anywhere you want!" Bonjo exclaimed, bringing out his inner 'hood.

There was a moment of silence on the phone, and

for a second Bonjo thought he had him reeled in. He yelled into the phone, "Hello! Hello!" The next thing he heard were JahJah's cries in the background. It shut him up real fast, hearing her beg for her life.

"Say goodbye to your bitch!" the voice said before the sound of a gun exploding rang through the phone.

The noise was so loud that Bonjo dropped the phone and stuck his finger in his ear. Everyone in the room heard the shot, and they knew that more than likely, whoever was on the other line had killed JahJah.

Emilia walked out of the room with her hands over her mouth in shock. Marcela just kept her head down, and LuLu was so mad that she let off a couple shots at the receiver on the floor.

Bonjo couldn't conceive what he'd just heard. He put his hands on top of his head in disbelief. He just lost his wife, and there was nothing he could do but swallow it.

Sosa finding a gun in Jamaica wasn't hard at all, considering she was already familiar with a few spots from the time she spent out there with Ox. She knew most of the back roads and the small villages deep inside of Kingston, so at no time would she ever become lost roaming around the Island. She understood the people as well, knowing but not crossing any boundaries.

Sonya finally pulled up to her house after a long day at work. She was tired as hell, and today she had delivered two babies in the hospital's emergency room. As she walked up to put her key in the front door, Sosa slid from behind the side of the house and walked right up on her before she could get the door open. Sonya started to scream out, but thought about the gun stuffed in the side of her gut. Yelling would only be sure death. What do you want?" she asked Sosa with fear in her eyes. "I don't have any money!"

"Just open the door real slowly. Is there anybody in the house?"

"No, I live alone," Sonya replied.

Once they entered the house, Sosa pushed Sonya onto the couch and peeked out of the window to see if anybody had seen her.

When she got a closer look at the woman with the gun, Sonya realized that it was the same woman from the hospital who was asking all the questions about her records. Right then, she knew the reason why she was there. As Sonya was the main person giving her the runaround, this wouldn't make things any better either.

"I'm not for the same games you played at the hospital, so please don't insult my intelligence. I'ma ask you some questions, and you need to tell me the truth or I swear by God, I'ma shoot you in the face, do you understand?" Sosa threatened before pulling up a chair and taking a seat in front of her.

Sonya nodded her head in agreement, sitting back on the couch with her pocketbook wrapped in her arms.

"Do you remember me?"

"Yeah, from the hospital earlier today. You…"

"Stop! I'm not talking about from today. Do you remember me from about eight years ago?" Sosa asked, staring her in the eyes.

Sonya didn't have to think about it. She knew exactly who Sosa was, but she wasn't sure if it was going to be safe to say that she remembered her, because she feared what might happen to her if she did. She hesitated for a moment before realizing that telling the truth might just save her life. It was a good thing that Sonya didn't try to lie, because Sosa remembered her clear as day as one of the nurses in the room when she was having the baby.

"I don't know your name, but I remember you," Sonya said weakly.

"Where is my daughter?" Sosa asked, getting right down to it.

"She died after you gave birth."

"That's a lie! Now tell me where my baby is!" Sosa repeated, taking the safety off the large .45 automatic.

The room was quiet, and Sonya just looked at Sosa and then at the gun. There was more to this story than what Sosa thought, and exposing the real dirt could be worse than the single issue at hand. The more she thought about it, Sonya was willing to take the bullet before letting out the hospital's secrets. "Me don't know not'ing," Sonya said, sitting up on the edge of the couch with a stern look in her eyes.

Sosa calmed that whole tough girl shit down with a single gunshot to Sonya's knee. The bullet ripped her knee halfway off, leaving a hole inside of it the size of a golf ball.

Sonya screamed in agonizing pain, holding on to what was left of her knee. "Crazy blood clot bitch!" she managed to say between screams.

Sosa placed the barrel of the gun on the tip of Sonya's chin and lifted her head up to face her. "I told you to stop playin' wit' me. I sat in front of ya house for two hours waiting for you, and none of ya neighbors are home to hear you scream. So, bitch, if you wanna live through tonight, you better start talking!" she warned.

There was yet another moment of silence in the room. Sosa really thought she was going to have to kill Sonya before she got a chance to find out what was going on.

Sonya on the other hand, didn't want to be shot again in any part of her body. All she wanted was for Sosa to leave. "Ox come and take ya baby. Him take any baby he want."

"Why? Why does he take the babies?" Sosa asked, not understanding.

"Him use the babies to run drugs to da States. Some babies live and some babies die," Sonya explained through her pain.

"So, what happened to my baby?"

"Me don't know. Ox took da girl. She was alive when he left wit' her."

Hearing what Ox was up to was blowing Sosa's mind. She could remember reading some shit like this in a book before but never did she think it happened in real life. *How many other women has he done this to, and how many people were in on the scam at the hospital?* She knew that Ox had money and power, but this was going way too far. It not only saddened Sosa but it angered her that people that did shit like this were still allowed to walk the Earth.

"How much do you get?" Sosa asked, only wanting to know if this was forced on her, or voluntary.

When Sonya put her head down in shame, Sosa already knew the answer. Sosa stood up. She was just about done with the whole ordeal. She pointed the gun at Sonya's head, thinking about all the little babies that may have died at her hands. She thought about the possibility of her daughter being one of the babies used for transport. She leaned forward so the gun was about a foot away from Sonya's face.

"Ask the doctor. Him know what happened to ya daughter," Sonya said as her last words.

Sosa squeezed the trigger, planting a bullet right in between her eyes and knocking her head back onto the couch. Blood, brain matter and skull fragments painted the wall behind the couch. Sosa took one last look at her before turning around and walking out of the house.

Chapter 9

Working in the coca field wasn't getting any easier for Semaj, who was winding down from another hot ass day. As she walked towards the factory that converted the coca leaves into cocaine powder, Vikingo, a factory worker called her name. This was the first time anyone even acknowledged her, other than Valentina. He sort of caught her by surprise, but after he walked over to her, the view was worth her waiting to see what he wanted.

Vikingo was a handsome, dark-skinned, 6'2" 235 pound Columbian that was cut up like an action figure. Semaj could see the ripples of his six-pack through his tank top, and could see the bulge of his manhood through his well-fitting jeans. His approach was kind, gentle and sweet as he walked up to her, took her hand and kissed the back of it. "*Hola, mamacita.* My name is Vikingo," he introduced himself with a smile that could melt even the coldest woman's heart.

Semaj blushed like a little schoolgirl at the sight of him standing before her. *I know it's been a while, but damn, this nigga could get it!* she thought to herself while holding eye contact. She practically forgot her name, being so caught up in his disarming aura. "My name is Semaj," she finally managed to say.

"I know who you are, but I just didn't know you were this beautiful. I mean, I heard the rumors from other workers about a woman working in the field that makes the sun jealous throughout the day."

Semaj laughed at his lil' game, having already heard the line before but in a different context. It was still cute coming off of his tongue though. He spoke good English, although it was hard hiding his Columbian accent. Trying to speak English only made his voice sound better.

"Well, *mami*, let me get that for you," he said, and grabbed the wheelbarrow full of plants she was pushing. You have a good evening!" he said, casually walking off pushing the wheelbarrow.

A feeling of disappointment crept up on Semaj when the handsome gentleman she just met vanished as quickly as he had appeared. His disappearing act made him more intriguing and she walked the entire way back to the compound with a smile on her face, thinking about how cute Vikingo was.

At times she'd wonder why she stayed on the compound this long, slaving and carrying on for very little money a day. What she was getting paid wasn't worth all that she was doing in the scorching heat. She often thought about leaving and going to London to find Qua, because she knew that he would be more than willing to take care of her. But after careful consideration, she knew that she had to make it on her own before she could be with anyone else. She was growing and maturing into a real woman, and taking responsibility for herself and for her actions. She didn't want Qua to rescue her she needed to rescue herself. He already done more than enough by saving her life and getting her out of Ox's estate when she revealed he was the enemy. Now it was time for Semaj to do things her way. No doubt, hustling was always going to be in her blood no matter what, and one way or another Semaj was going to get back on top where she belonged.

Before she made it to the end of the road, Valentina pulled up on her in a golf cart and stopped her in her tracks. Valentina could tell that Semaj was exhausted and figured she'd offer her a ride. But it wasn't going to be back to the compound. She wanted to take some time out to dig deeper into Semaj's mindset. "Get in," she said, motioning with a nod of her head.

Semaj got in, and Valentina drove the cart for a while until she drove so far away from the compound that Semaj couldn't see it any more. The first thing that came to Semaj's mind was that she was about to get whacked. She started thinking about things that she did in her life that may have violated Valentina in some way. Valentina didn't say anything during the entire ride, and when the cart came to a stop Semaj noticed that they were in the middle of nowhere. *This would be the perfect place to kill me too,* she thought to herself

She turned to Valentina. "What's going on?" she

asked her with a curious look on her face and not sure what to expect.

"Let me ask you this, Semaj. What have you accomplished in your life that you can say benefited you towards your future?"

The question caught Semaj off guard, but as she took a moment to think about it nothing she had done up to this point in her life was worth mentioning. She was somewhat of a boss for a few months until the Milano Family broke up. But Semaj was brought into a family that was already established in the business so whether it failed or succeeded she couldn't take credit.

"Well, since you can't answer that, then answer me this. What do you want out of life?" she asked with a sincere look in her eyes and wanting a sincere response from Semaj.

"Honestly, I want to be like you," Semaj replied as she turned to face Valentina. She and Semaj held eye contact for a moment before Valentina looked off into the open field.

They both sat there and enjoyed the setting sun while conversing about goals and Semaj's plans for the future. It was ironic how Valentina could see herself in Semaj in many different aspects of her life. There was so much that Valentina had to offer the young woman, but the most important thing she wanted to give her but couldn't was wisdom. That was something that only came with age. For now, knowledge and understanding would have to do, and that in itself was something beneficial, if

Semaj knew how to use it.

"But I shot da bitch in her face with a .357!" Paris said, walking down the steps with Ox following right behind her. She sat down on the living room couch and just stared at the floor in disbelief at the fact that Ox just told her that Semaj might still be alive. Paris knew this all along, but she had to play the stupid role so it didn't look like she was deceiving Ox.

Ox was hot too. He was walking throughout the house yelling and throwing things around like a madman. The Milano Family was his worst enemy, and he hated every last one of them with a passion. Just when he thought that he cut the heads of the family off, one got through the cracks. He wasn't worried about Bonjo and the Milano Hitters because none of them were leaders, but it was Semaj that had become and still was a threat. She had proved that she could be a nigga's worst nightmare. She was pretty, and she knew how to hustle; two qualities that could be deadly if a bitch knew how to use them. With somebody like her, the war would never end between the Milano's and the Jamaicans.

"I'ma finish it!" Paris stood up, stopping Ox in his tracks as he paced across the room. "You're stressing over nothing. I fucked up, but I'ma fix it," she assured him in an effort to calm him down.

"Naw, me gon' finish it me-self!" he said, pushing her hands down and away from his waist.

He tried to walk off, but she stood in front of him, blocking his path. Ox wasn't trying to hear anything she was talking about right now, and getting in his way wasn't a smart move for Paris. He looked at her and asked her calmly to move out his way. It was so calm that it scared her. She stepped aside and watched him go upstairs to grab his things.

Paris didn't know what he was going to do, but one thing was for sure; she would be home on babysitting duty for Nyala again until he got back, which was something she had unwillingly become accustom to doing.

Dr. Hunter walked into the room and was startled by Sosa standing in the corner of his office and looking out of the window. He hesitantly came in and closed the door behind him, not knowing the reason why she was there. "Can I help you with something?" he asked her with a confused look on his face.

Sosa wasted no time in pulling the .45 from the back of her waistband and placing it down by her side.

Dr. Hunter looked at her and then looked at the gun, and walked over to his desk like he wasn't impressed by the gun.

When he took a seat, Sosa walked around to the

front of the desk, keeping her eyes on him the entire time in case he wanted to play hero. She gave him some time to take in her face, hoping that he would remember her without her having to say a word.

It took him a few moments, but it finally dawned on him who she was. It had been a long time, and he thought that Ox had killed her by now, being as though he hadn't seen her since the day he took her daughter from her. Even after realizing who she was, he still wasn't up for volunteering any information.

The one thing he couldn't do was play stupid with a woman that remembered every face from that day, and Sosa could still see his black ass reaching out and grabbing her baby when she delivered her.

"I know you probably don't have records of me having my baby here, but you're gonna answer one question for me. And if you don't, I swear by God I'ma put a bullet smack dab in the middle of ya head," Sosa said calmly.

"You think you gonna shoot me and just walk out of here alive? You won't make—"

"Where is my baby?" she asked, cutting him off and getting the ball rolling.

Dr. Hunter could see that Sosa wasn't playing any games, and she was there with a premeditated thought about the outcome of this encounter. By the way she clutched the gun in her hand, it was obvious that she was serious, and doing saying anything other than what she wanted to know would end his life. He didn't even have to think twice about this as he looked into her eyes and saw her determination to find her daughter.

"Can I?" the doctor asked, pointing over to the file cabinets.

She motioned for him to do it. He slowly walked over to the drawers with his hands visible so she wouldn't think he was trying to grab a gun or something. He pulled one of the doors open and searched for a second before grabbing a folder that had Nyala's name on it. "He brings her in for regular checkups," he said, setting the folder on the table. "Her name is Nyala Jennings. Look, I'm sorry bout ya kid, but Ox… him crazy!"

Sosa wasn't trying to hear what the doctor was talking about. He had answered her question, and it was no longer necessary for him to even breathe any more. She raised the gun and pointed it at his head.

The doctor sat back in his chair like she didn't have the guts to pull the trigger. It was the middle of the day, and hundreds of people were outside of his door. *There's no way she could be that stupid!* he thought to himself.

Dr. Hunter didn't get a chance to say another word as Sosa released two hollow-point bullets into his chest, knocking him back in his chair. He gasped for air as the bullets entered his chest and exited out is back. He took his final breaths staring into the eyes of Sosa.

The two gunshots got the attention of the medical staff that was moving around in the hallway outside of his office.

The hospital's security made it up to the room in

seconds, armed and trained to handle problems such as this. The bystanders in the hallway let security know that nobody had exited the room since the two shots went off, so they figured that the shooter was still inside. They kicked the doctor's door in with their weapons drawn, and entered with itchy trigger fingers.

Unfortunately, there was nobody but Dr. Hunter in the office, dead in his chair with his eyes still open. The office window was wide open, and when one of the security guards went to look out of it, there were no signs of anyone.

The window was only on the second floor, so Sosa had planned her exit the moment she set foot in the office. She was gone with the wind, with the medical records in her hand.

Qua had been trying to get in contact with Semaj for the past week or so. It was like she had disappeared into thin air. Her cell phone had been shut off, so there was no way for him to reach out to her. Besides not knowing whether she was dead or alive, he had run out of work and needed to re-up ASAP.

"You got some mail," Kayla smiled, coming into his office with a handful of envelopes. After placing them down she wrapped her arms around Qua's shoulders.

Kayla was like the secretary of the club who took care of a lot of the financial aspects of the business, like paying bills and making sure they stayed stocked with liquor and food. She had also become Qua's flirt buddy by default.

"Not right now, Kayla," Qua huffed, shrugging her arms off of him.

"What's wrong did I do something?"

"No, I just have a lot of shit on my mind and I don't feel like being bothered."

Kayla was definitely an asset to Qua but he had made the mistake of mixing business with pleasure. Although he hadn't slept with Kayla he flirted with her enough to give her hope that she had a chance with him. She was well aware he was in love with another woman but what she felt she had on her side was that she was there and the other woman was not.

"Is there anything I can help you with? You know talking to me always makes you feel better," she said seductively caressing the side of his face.

"What part of I don't feel like being bothered did you not understand," Qua stated, grabbing Kayla's hand and removing it from his face. With the foul mood he was in, he didn't even want to be bothered with her today. "Yo, if anybody comes through here tell them I'm not here," Qua told her, and looked down at the newspaper.

There was a lot going on in his mind, and the main thing was finding some coke before niggas started looking for it somewhere else. The 16 Tent meeting wasn't scheduled for another two weeks, and that was way too long for the streets of London to be dry. The sound of the phone ringing snapped Qua out of the pissy ass trance he found himself in. He was expecting a very important phone call, and hoped this was it.

"Yo!" Qua answered.

"Won, boy! I'm at the airport. Come get me," Ox said into the phone as the jet taxied off the runway.

This wasn't the call that Qua was waiting for, and he wondered why Ox was in London.

Technically, it was a little too early for him to be coming to collect his money from the bricks he fronted Qua, and if he was there for that, it would really put a kink in Qua's plan for using Ox's money to buy the largest amount of cocaine he could at the 16 Tent meeting. Qua and Jeramie's money alone wasn't long enough, and five hundred bricks was the least anybody could buy at the meeting, no exceptions.

"Look, I gotta go. I'll be back in a couple of hours," Qua told Kayla after he hung up the phone. He noticed she was standing off to the side with a look of hurt written on her face. At that moment a feeling of guilt hit Qua, realizing he was wrong for being so dismissive towards her. Kayla had been a rock for him not only with business but she would also listen when he had moments of weakness missing Semaj.

"That's fine," Kayla said, putting her head down.

"Listen, why don't we have dinner tonight. Make the reservations."

"Really!" Within an instant Kayla's frown turned into a smile.

"Yes. Text me the information and I'll be there. Gotta go," Qua said, kissing Kayla on her forehead before leaving his office, in route to pick Ox up.

Chapter 10

Murda Mitch counted a little more than two million dollars out of the money he took from out Gio's safe. The coke he took from Marcela sat on the dresser untouched. For the mission he was on, he didn't need to get high. He had a natural high within himself. He really didn't even need the money he took, considering that fact that he knew he wasn't going to be alive to spend all of it.

He looked at himself in the mirror, seeing the damage Gio had done to his face and his body during the months of torture he had to endure. Gio was a sick mufucka on the low, and some of the shit he did to Murda Mitch only could be seen on TV. His face was permanently disfigured from the countless blows it took from punches, and his neck carried a 360-degree rope burn around it from Gio repeatedly hanging him from the ceiling until he was almost dead. Cigar burns covered his entire upper body and third degree lighter burns had melted two of his fingers to the point where they had become nubs. He still hadn't cut his hair, and it looked like it was starting to lock up into dreads.

He just sat on the bed looking at all the money, and realized that it wasn't taking away the pain. There was no amount of money in the world that could ease the pain of losing Semaj, his lone reason for living, and the only flesh and blood that remained of Kasey, the woman who was buried with his heart.

What the Milano Family took away from him was bigger than the Mafia, and the killings were never going to end. Mitch wasn't going to rest until every member of the Milano Family was dead and buried six feet under with his daughter.

Semaj walked into a section of the house where everyone went to watch TV or do family activities. When she got to the room, it seemed like everybody that lived on the compound was there. She quickly turned around in an attempt to leave, not wanting to interrupt their family time.

"Semaj!" Valentina called to her, stopping her in her tracks.

Semaj didn't notice that she was in the room, and that was because she sat smack in the middle of the crowd. There had to be about twenty-five adults and twenty children in the room. Semaj turned around, and it seemed like all eyes were on her. In fact, all eyes were on her, and everybody was silent once Valentina spoke.

An adorable little girl no more than four years old walked over to Semaj, grabbed her by the hand and guided her over to Valentina.

"I didn't mean to intrude," Semaj said, looking around at everybody who was still staring at her.

Valentina smiled, grabbed Semaj by the hand and sat her down. She didn't have any idea what was going on, and Valentina didn't make it any easier, sitting there with a grin on her face. What she was about to tell her would change her life. Valentina reached beside her pillow and grabbed a small box and took out a photo album. Semaj had a confused look on her face, wondering where she was going with all this.

"I want to tell all of you a story," Valentina announced to everyone in the room.

Those that were standing took a seat on the floor, and those that were already sitting just got more comfortable. Semaj also got comfortable, honored that she was going to be able to sit and listen to a family story.

"Many, many years ago, a woman by the name of Maria Espriella met a wonderful, sweet, charming and very handsome man. They fell in love and were together for quite some time until their parents found out about their relationship. It was completely forbidden for the two different cultures to mix, but Maria ran off with him, and they lived happily together for a while. During the time that they lived together, a child was conceived and Maria gave birth to a beautiful baby girl and named her Natia."

"One day, Maria was out shopping for groceries when she stumbled across her father. He immediately grabbed her and forced her to return back to their home. Maria was afraid that if her father knew about the baby, he would probably end up killing the baby and the baby's father. So for that reason alone she never mentioned it to anyone for the protection of her family."

"After a while, she tried to go back to find her husband and the baby, but he and baby Natia were gone. Maria heard nothing from them for years."

"As time went on, Maria found her daughter and her husband, along with his new wife living a whole other life. On the day she found her husband, they both decided to allow their child to come of age before they broke the news to her about who her true mother was. Maria vowed to always look out for her daughter as much as she could, often watching her from afar."

"Time went on, and eventually Maria moved on with her life, marrying and having several children by the most powerful man in Columbia..."

Some of the children in the room had already fallen asleep by the time Valentina got to this part of her story. But for everybody else, the story was intriguing. It sounded like a Columbian love story, and Semaj was all ears, wanting to hear the rest of the story.

Valentina continued:

"One day many years later, Natia had a baby, and Maria's old husband told her about this, giving Maria the option to see her and be a part of both Natia's and her granddaughter's life. Maria loved the idea, so she planned for the trip. An unexpected tragic event occurred, and Natia was killed. Her granddaughter was then taken away by the father before Maria could even see her…"

Valentina could barely tell the story at this point because she had begun to cry, something no one had ever seen her do. Semaj was already in tears by the time she told the part about Natia being killed. She could feel Valentina's pain and that resonated with Semaj. She sat attentively and continued to listen.

"One day, Maria met a girl… a girl that reminded her so much of her daughter, Natia. She looked into her eyes and knew right then and there that the girl standing before her was Natia's daughter. She was a princess, a Mafia Princess, and Maria vowed never to let her out of her sight," Valentina finished.

The story had a couple people in the room teary eyed, and Valentina had to take a moment to get herself together.

Semaj was also in tears thinking about her mother and how much she missed her. She looked around the room at the people who were looking down at her with smiles on their faces. "I don't understand," she said with a confused look on her face.

Valentina opened one of the photo albums and started showing Semaj pictures of her mother and of her when she was a baby. Despite the separation, Gio made sure he always sent her pictures. She even had pictures of

Kasey when she was a baby.

"My name is Maria Valentina Espriella and your mother, Natia Kataleena Espriella was my daughter. You are my granddaughter, Semaj," Valentina said and grabbed Semaj's hand and pulled her closer to her. "I have been waiting for this moment for so long, my princess!" she cried.

Semaj couldn't believe it. She was always under the impression that her grandmother died from cancer. To now find out her real grandmother was still alive was almost unimaginable to her. And not only was she alive, but she was one of the world's largest cocaine distributors and Columbia's head honcho. The people in the room began to embrace the newest addition to their family, happier than ever to finally have her home.

Chapter 11

Ox was in the passenger seat of the Benz while Qua drove through the city looking for a place to party tonight. Ox hadn't even been there for a day, and he was already ready to confront Qua about what happened to his son. He was waiting for the right time to do it just in case he had to put a bullet in his head. It was one in the morning on a Thursday, and they were in the middle of nowhere. Ox felt this was the perfect opportunity to not only find out about his son, but to see what was going on between Qua and the Milano Family.

"Pull over right chere," Ox pointed, directing Qua to a parking lot in a strip mall.

Qua pulled over while checking out the area and his surroundings before parking in front of a closed dental office. He immediately stuck his left hand into his jacket pocket where he rested it on a .40 cal, already on point to what he thought Ox might be up to. There wasn't a soul outside, so it would be nothing for Qua to put a bullet in Ox's head and pull off without any witnesses.

However, the thing Qua wasn't aware of was that Ox had his right hand tucked into his pocket, clutching the same kind of gun. He was holding onto it the entire time they were driving, debating whether or not he should shoot him off of GP.

"Me wanna holla at chu about a couple t'ings, broad" Ox said, taking a puff of the ganja he was blowing. "I like you, Qua, and that's prob'ly de only reason I talking to you right now. If you was anybody else, I woulda been killed you by now, no question. And me damn sure not afraid of death," he said, looking down at Qua's hand to let him know that he knew Qua was strapped.

"So, what's up, Ox? Get down to it," Qua said, wanting to hear what he had to say but really not in the mood for any shoot 'em up, bang-bang talk.

"What happened to me son?" Ox asked with a serious look in his eyes.

Qua looked at Ox like he had just insulted him. The question alone made him want to fire off a round or two at Ox through his jacket right then and there, but he didn't. He thought fast on his feet like he always did, thinking of how he could get rid of two problems at once. He turned to Ox with a stern look in his eyes and said, "Man, look. I wasn't goin' to tell you this until I was sure the intel I got was official. I was gonna kill da nigga myself, because I think he's the one that killed my lil' man, Nasah. It's a mufucka out here named Jeramie. Da nigga swears he owns shit. I think his peoples is the Abbott Family. Anyway, word was supposed to have got back to him that Rude-Boy was the one who did it. Niggas is saying Jeramie killed ya son right after Pelpa was murdered," Qua lied.

As bad as the lie seemed, it didn't sound too far out there for Ox not to believe it. The Jamaicans and the Abbott Family had been beefing for a while, and that scenario could have easily taken place, even though Qua knew it was a complete lie. Qua knew that if Ox even thought Jeramie killed his son, he was going to put him in the ground for good. Qua already had the location to the next 16 Tent meeting, and he had a nice amount of money to get his foot in the door. If Jeramie wasn't that hard to get to, Qua probably would have killed him himself. But because Jeramie had a good security squad, it would be a power move to leave it up to the one Jamaican, Don Dada that could take on a small army by himself if he had to.

Qua sold the hell out of his Jeramie story because Ox ate it up. Ox started asking a lot of questions about Jeramie's whereabouts and what his security looked like. Qua even tried to insist that he be the one to put a bullet in his head, but Ox was determined to do it himself.

For a minute it got quiet in the car. Qua was ready to start the car so he could pull out of the lot, but Ox stopped him, sticking his arm out before he could put the car in drive. "I almost forgot, brada. Who was da girl you had at the whorehouse?" Ox asked, bringing back the tension that had left the car.

Qua gripped the gun tighter, thinking that Ox was

trying to rock him to sleep. Ox never did take his hand off his gun, so it remained pointed in his direction. There wasn't a lie Qua could come up with fast enough, so he told the truth… somewhat. "Oh, that was some bitch I used to fuck wit' back in New York. She got into something back in the city and asked me to come get her. Da bitch ended up leaving the Island before I could get back to her," he said with the attitude like he really didn't care about her.

"You know her people?" Ox asked, trying to see if Qua knew that he was beefing with the Milano family.

"I had da bitch when she was a buck. I tried to put her into some movies. The only nigga I knew from her family was her pops, Murda Mitch. He's a mafuckin' legend in the 'hood," Qua said while he kept his finger on the trigger in case Ox wasn't buying it.

Telling part of the truth helped him out big time, because it saved him from getting shot. Had he given any other story, Ox would have finished him. So for now, Qua was in the clear, but the slight look Ox gave him let Qua know that this wasn't going to be the end of this inquiry. Hopefully by the time Ox put everything together, it would be too late.

Semaj still couldn't believe that she had another family that she never knew about as she sat in her room looking at the many photo albums that Valentina gave to her. Later on tonight she was supposed to sit down and meet everybody in the Espriella family, learning their names and what positions they had in the family business. The sound of Valentina's golf cart pulling up outside of her window prompted her to glance outside.

"Take a ride with me," Valentina yelled up to Semaj, who was standing there in a flowery dress, a pair of sandals and a big straw hat.

Semaj complied, putting away the album and meeting Valentina outside. She got in the cart and they drove a good distance. At a certain point during the ride, Semaj noticed things that were familiar to her. By the time they reached their destination, she knew where she was. It was the same place Valentina took her to when Semaj thought she was about to be killed. There was a crowd of people standing out there when they pulled up, and one in particular person stood out; Vikingo.

"You were like a missing piece to a puzzle, Semaj, and now that you're here, our family is complete," Valentina said, getting out of the golf cart.

They walked over to the open land and looked out at about two square miles of dirt. The last time Semaj was up here it was all grass. Confused yet again, she didn't know what was going on or what was about to happen.

"This will be your coca field," Valentina said, shocking the hell out of her. "I will teach you how to grow your own cocaine. After that, you will learn how to manufacture it and then... well, you should know what to do with it after that."

My own cocaine field! Semaj thought to herself. Just like everything else that happened thus far, she just found it hard to believe. Everything was happening all too fast. It seemed like just yesterday she was on all fours, planting seeds and pulling weeds from a coca field, and now Valentina was sitting here telling her that she was going to be growing her own coke. "Why me?" she asked, curious as to why she was being treated this way. "You have all these children and grandchildren. They don't have their own coca fields," she stated with a confused look on her face.

Valentina walked up to Semaj and grabbed her hand. "In this family, the business gets passed down from generation to generation in the correct order. That's how it's been since the beginning. Your mother was my first child and you are my first grandchild, which makes you the inheritor of the family business and next to head the family," Valentina explained to her.

It was still all too confusing for Semaj to understand. She just looked out at the open field, then back at the crowd of about twenty people standing off to the side. She shook her head in disbelief, and for the first time tears of happiness filled her eyes. "So, who are all these people?" she asked, pointing over at the crowd.

"Oh, those are your field workers. For this small field you only need about twenty of them. They work for one thousand dollars a day, five days a week, which will be nothing compared to how much you'll make after the field starts producing. That's the reason why I put you in the field when you first got here. I wanted you to know and respect what the field workers have to go through daily. They work very hard, and you of all people should know that very well!" She smiled, thinking about the night she found Semaj in bed sleep with all her clothes on after working her first day in the field.

Semaj stood there and listened to everything Valentina was schooling her on about the cocaine farming process. Valentina warned her about poachers that often tried to steal coca plants from the field, and the price for keeping the Columbian police from bothering her. She put her onto a lot of things as they both sat there and watched the workers get started on cleaning and planting in the field. It was a lot, but Valentina had to teach Semaj everything there was to know about the cocaine game, knowing that one day she would have to step up and be the head of the family.

When LuLu wanted to, she could rock the hell out of a pair of jeans and some heels. She had a cute baby face with dimples, and hair that came to the center of her back. She was short, with a pair of thick thighs that complemented her fat ass and a toned stomach that highlighted her tiny waist. Besides being overly aggressive with a gun, LuLu was bad.

The club was packed, and LuLu popped bottle after bottle in the VIP section, by herself. At times her drunk ass would get up on the table and dance seductively when one of her favorite songs would come on. She was solo, so it didn't matter. LuLu hadn't had fun like this in a while, shit, she was having even more fun partying by herself and not having to worry about always protecting Semaj and Gio.

LuLu was probably the only one that was not afraid to leave the house. Tonight she had plans on hitting the club and having some fun, and she'd be dammed if she had to go with a bunch of security. She was arrogant and she had every right to be. She was a stone cold killer and was thirsty to put in some work after all the people in her family that had been murdered. Bonjo was worried about the nigga that was out there snatching his people up, but the nigga who was doing it needed to be worried about her!

"When you gonna call me, ma?" the nigga she had been talking to asked when they got outside of the club after it closed.

"I'ma call you," LuLu smiled, turning away and walking off.

When she walked off, the nigga watched as her ass swayed from side to side, jiggling with every switch.

She walked towards the parking lot where her Dodge Charger was and popped her trunk with the remote on her key chain. She threw her pocketbook inside and pulled out her jacket, tossing it over her shoulders. The weight of the compact .45 automatic bounced against her side when she put her jacket on. Looking around, it was like the party had spilled over into the parking lot because a lot of people were out there blasting their car radios and talking to females. LuLu looked on, happy to be able to have fun for a change.

She went to reach for her car door and felt the presence of someone standing behind her. Instinctively she reached in her pocket like she was grabbing her keys, but instead latched on to her gun. She didn't even get a chance to pull it out, feeling the pressure of a barrel being pressed against her lower back.

"Be stupid and I'ma blow ya fucking back out!" Mitch said, and opened the door for her. "Get in!" he demanded, trying to push her in.

She wasn't budging, and instead put up a little resistance. There was no way she was getting into the car, even if she had a gun. If he was going to do anything, it had to be done right there. All she needed was just a little space to work with, but Mitch was so close up on her that the hand she had on her gun was pressed up against the side of the back door window. She could feel his warm breath on her neck as he pushed her into the car. She fell on the driver's seat, and when she looked up his gun was pointed in her face. Shooting now would only end in her death and probably an injury to his leg. She needed more.

"My man, is there a problem?" the nigga from the club said as he and a group of his boys walked past, noticing that something didn't look right with LuLu.

Mitch didn't bother to respond to the guy, but when he walked up on him, he had no other choice. He turned his gun on dude and squeezed off a round, shooting him in his stomach.

LuLu took that opportunity and let off several shots, hitting Mitch in his body. Before falling to the ground, Mitch let off into the driver's side of the car, but only striking LuLu in her arm. She got out of the vehicle, looking for the shooter who had ducked behind the car after taking shots at her. She froze at the sight of Murda Mitch lying on the ground, looking up at her with the gun still in his hand. He pointed it at her like he was about to shoot, but LuLu dipped back off to the front of the car, unable to get her shot off.

It was pandemonium. The crowd of people in the parking lot dispersed, running for cover behind cars.

Murder Mitch! she thought to herself as she backed away from the car with her gun pointed in his direction. *I thought this nigga was dead already!*

One thing she wasn't going to do was stick around to find out why he was trying to snatch her. She grew up seeing the work he had put in for Gio, and the chance of him wearing a vest was more than likely. If she could get away now, that would have been the best thing for her and she knew it. She took off through the parking lot with her arm still leaking blood from the gunshot.

Mitch eventually got up and made it to his car. Getting shot one time with a vest on wasn't that bad, but getting hit multiple times at close range knocked the wind out of him. He wanted to chase LuLu down and put a bullet in her head, but when he looked around she was nowhere in sight and all he could hear in the distance was the sounds of sirens.

LuLu must have been toting something more than a gun with her this time. She must've had and Angel sitting on her shoulder, because Mitch never failed when it came down to putting work in.

Qua finally dropped Ox back off at his hotel after a long night of talking. It pretty much took up his whole day being with him. He missed the dinner he was supposed to have with Kayla, but he thought about her all night. He couldn't understand why it took him this long not laying pipe to her. As he thought about it Qua did know and her name was Semaj. Kayla was cute, smart and had a body out of this world but his heart belonged to another woman. But Qua had needs and Kayla seemed like a safe bet. He hardly ever saw her talking to or associating with other men, and just the thought of that made him wonder if she was getting any dick at all.

He pulled up to her condo on the east side of the city, hoping that she would be home. Looking down at his watch he saw that it was three in the morning, and knew for sure that if she was home, most likely she would be sleep. He dialed her number anyway, taking a shot at it.

The phone just kept ringing until her answering machine came on. He wasn't going to give up that easy and decided to call again. She didn't answer this time either. *I'ma try one more time, and if she don't answer, I'm out,* Qua thought to himself, looking up at her window. The phone rang and rang again, and Qua was just about to hang up, but Kayla answered. The constant ringing woke her out of her sleep.

"Hello," she answered in a groggy voice.

"Come open the door," Qua said, stepping out of the car, happy as shit that she answered.

"Fuck you, Qua! I don't feel like playin' around wit' you!" she shot back with an attitude, damn near about to hang up in his ear.

"I'm sorry about dinner. Let me make it up to you," he said as he walked up the steps that led to her spot. "I got caught up. Just come to the door."

The phone went dead. Kayla had hung up, but by the time he got up the steps, he could hear the door locks being opened. She opened the door and stood to the side and let him in. He could see the frustration in her eyes as he walked past her. The bathrobe she had on was wrapped tightly, only showing off a little bit of her cleavage. He followed her as she walked into the kitchen, grabbed a bottle of water out of the refrigerator and slammed the refrigerator door.

"Don't be mad at me," he said, grabbing her arm before she got the chance to walk off. "Come here." He pulled her closer to him.

"Come on, Qua. I don't feel like playing around wit' you right now. You fuckin' left me in that restaurant for hours by myself, and you pop up three at the morning. For what?" she snapped.

"Come 'ere. Didn't I say I was sorry?" he said, softly wrapping his arms around her waist. "I'll give you the day off tomorrow and I'll send you shopping," he joked, grabbing her chin and turning her to face him.

His touch along with the way he looked into her eyes made it hard for her to stay mad at him. He reached in to undo her robe, curious as to what she looked like under it, but she jumped back with a smile on her face and shook her head no.

He played the game with her, already knowing where this was headed. He grabbed her arm and pulled her closer to him again, with a sexy, seductive look in his eyes.

Kayla couldn't resist very much standing in front of the man she'd been fantasizing about damn near every night. This time when he reached in to grab the belt to her robe, she let him. He untied the belt. She didn't have anything on underneath it, and her body looked amazing. His dick instantly got rock hard, and when he looked up at her, she had a sexy, seductive smile on her face. He wrapped his arms back around her waist, pulled her body close to him and planted a slow, soft, passionate kiss on her lips.

"I want cheese eggs…" he said and kissed her again. Turkey bacon… he kissed. Home fries… he kissed. And three pancakes," he kissed, all the while backing her up to her bedroom.

"I'm not cooking you no breakfast!" she giggled, catching on to what Qua was demanding ahead of time.

"Yes, you will. I promise you will," he replied, and slammed the bedroom door behind them.

"Semaj, please come here," Valentina announced, catching her before she had left the house.

Semaj was on her way to meet up with Vikingo, who had invited her to have dinner with him in town. They were becoming closer each day, and the Espriella family was also beginning to embrace her more. This was going to be her first trip off the compound since she'd been there, and being as though this was her day off she was planning on enjoying it to the utmost before having to go back to work after the weekend. She didn't have any idea what Valentina wanted and hoped that whatever it was could wait. "Yes?" she answered as she entered the living room where Valentina was standing and playing with her bird through the cage.

"Have a seat," she said, not even turning to look at her. "I want you to travel to Miami with Jorge. The Haitians are looking for a new supplier and I want you to negotiate a deal on my behalf. Your uncle will fill you in on everything when you get there. Do we understand each other?" she asked in more of a demanding way while still not taking her eyes off the bird.

Semaj understood her very clearly. Whatever Valentina asked her to do at this point was pretty much getting done, no questions asked. Through everything she had schooled Semaj on about the drug game, making a deal with the Haitians didn't sound that bad. Plus, it was going to give Semaj the opportunity to show her negotiating skills. They were going to be needed if she was going to last under the Espriella roof, even if she was the long lost granddaughter.

Chapter 12

Sosa sat in the back of an old shack, strapping up to get ready to start a small war. She'd purchased as much ammo as she could throughout the day, along with a used vest and a homemade silencer that she prayed to God worked. She could have easily gone and purchased these items brand new, but it wouldn't have been a smart idea. She would probably have been dead before she got a chance to use them. The streets were the best and the safest place to get the things she needed without bringing any attention to herself.

Sosa felt like a commando. She didn't even know if she was going to make it out of Ox's compound alive, let alone with her daughter who might not even want to come with her. But at this point, Sosa was willing to take her chances…anything for her seed.

Even though she was somewhat familiar with the compound, there were some things that had changed, maybe even for the better. The only way she could get into the compound was by going in through a blind spot, a place where the cameras didn't go. But the only problem with that was the fact a heavily armed guard was there, ready for whatever.

Sosa felt like it was now or never as she headed down the back road where the blind spot was. She could see the guard standing outside and looking around attentively. "Please, God, let this silencer work!" she prayed, clutching the .45 in her hoodie pocket. The closer she got to the guard, the more she became scared. Her palms were sweating and her heart was racing, and it seemed like the guard kept his eyes on her as she approached.

She had to be about ten yards away by now. She took one hand out of her pocket to remove her hood, and once the guard saw that it was a female, he eased up a little and turned his head to look down the road in the opposite direction. That was all she needed.

She pulled the gun from her pocket and pointed it right at his head. By the time he turned back around with the large assault rifle in his hand, she was already squeezing the trigger. The single round knocked a chunk out his head and dropped him instantly. The shot wasn't loud, but it definitely wasn't silenced like an official silencer. She looked around to see if the noise caused any commotion, which it didn't. She dragged his body off to the side so nobody would happen to stumble across it and sound the alarm.

Once inside the compound, the side door was her best option, because it would sometimes stay open for the guards. Being as though Ox wasn't home, there was no need for the guards to do as many rounds as they would if he was there, but the side door was still open.

She got into the house and noticed in the living room, two of Ox's guards were sitting in front of the TV playing soccer on the PlayStation. She treaded across the room like a ghost, walked right up behind them and fired a single bullet into each of their heads.

The gunshot sounded louder inside the house, and it got the attention of another guard who was sitting in the kitchen talking to his partner. He ran to the living room where he saw Sosa with the gun in her hand and the two Rastas slumped over on the couch. He began gunning at her with the large M-16, trying his best to take her head off.

The guard that was with him followed suit, coming out of the kitchen squeezing a .45 automatic.

Sosa sidestepped to the other end of the room, firing the last of the bullets in her gun before tossing it to the ground. She reached in her back pocket and pulled out the twin Glock .40 cals, and fired down on the two Jamaicans. They both got low and ducked for cover, taking refuge behind the couch and an entertainment system.

Sosa ran behind the mini bar firing both guns at the same time, and striking the Jamaican that ducked behind the entertainment system. The other Jamaican started yelling out words in a lingo that Sosa didn't understand, but she knew that he was calling for help.

"Now or never!" she yelled to herself. She jumped up from behind the mini bar firing at the Jake behind the couch as she walked up on him.

The sound of all the gunfire downstairs woke Paris up out of her sleep. She was scared as hell, not knowing what was going on and who was doing all the shooting. She ran to the closet and grabbed a Mack-11 and a vest from Ox's arsenal, and threw the vest over her head without even getting dressed. All she had on was the vest, a bra, and some boy shorts.

Sosa dropped both clips and popped two more in, hesitantly walking to the front of the house after killing the other Jamaican behind the couch.

The last of the guards that was standing outside had come in through the back way after hearing his boy calling out for him. He walked past the dead bodies in the living room and spotted Sosa at the front of the house. He started chopping at her with an AK-47, and at the same time Paris was creeping down the steps with the Mack-11.

The K forced Sosa to run the only place she could, which was up the steps. She saw a figure coming down the steps with a gun, but she didn't give a second thought in letting the 40's go when she got to the steps.

Paris was shocked to see Sosa running up the steps, and before she could let the Mack-11 ring, she took a bullet to the vest. Another bullet struck the very top of her shoulder, going in and out the back, but causing her to stumble backwards. She fell back into the bathroom, but not before sending Sosa a 12-pack of bullets that forced her to take cover behind a wall.

The guard from downstairs crept up the steps, not knowing where Sosa was. She was standing in the dark hallway, watching him until he got to the top of the steps. He didn't even feel the bullet entering his head as it sent him falling back down the stairs.

Sosa knew that it was time to get the hell out of the house before more guards decided to show up. She started opening door after door as she walked down the hallway in search of Nyala.

When she got to Nyala's bedroom and opened the door, she was sitting on her bed crying and holding her Barbie. "Sshhh!" Sosa hushed her as she slowly walked into the room and knelt down next to her bed.

This was the moment she had been waiting for what seemed like forever. She put down one gun and tucked the other one in her back pocket to show Nyala that she wasn't there to hurt her. She didn't want to do anything that would scare the little girl and make it any more difficult then what it was. "Hi, Nyala!" she said in a sweet voice as she knelt in front of her. "I'm your Mommy. I came to take you home with me. You wanna come home with me?" she asked in the gentlest voice she could muster up.

Nyala stared in her eyes for what seemed like an eternity. It was like the little girl was searching Sosa's soul for the truth and clearly she found it. Nyala stopped crying and nodded her head yes, and got up off the bed in an attempt to climb into Sosa's arms.

The Mack-11 might have jammed up on her while she was in the bathroom, but Paris wasn't out of weapons. She stormed into the room with the army knife that was strapped to the vest and raised it above her head.

Sosa saw her coming towards her through Nyala's mirror, but she moved out the way just a little too late. The large knife jammed into the back of Sosa's shoulder, sending an excruciating pain through her body. Paris went to strike her again, but Sosa had turned around and grabbed the arm the knife was in. She started punching Paris in her face as she held onto her arm as tightly as she could. The punches were accurate, but they didn't seem to faze Paris too much.

Suddenly, Paris dropped the knife and tried to jerk away from Sosa. Sosa let her arm go, and then dropped to the floor after hearing a gunshot go off.

Little Nyala had picked up the gun from the floor and was trying to shoot Paris. The bullets went everywhere, and the gun jerked out of her hand, but she did give it a try.

This gave Sosa enough time to pull out the gun she had in her back pocket and shoot at Paris, but Paris was already out of the room. She had run back into the bathroom where she locked the door, wrapped a towel around her shoulder and tried to un-jam the Mack-11.

Sosa turned and scooped Nyala up with one arm while pointing the .40 in front of her with the other hand as she walked down the hall and down the steps.

On her way through the house, she stopped at the mini bar and put Nyala down. She grabbed the lighter out of her pocket, looked around for a piece of paper, lit it and tossed it into the broken bottles of alcohol. They ignited immediately, sending flames straight to the ceiling.

She picked Nyala back up and jetted out of the same side door she came in through.

Chapter 13

Qua woke up to the smell of bacon, eggs and home fries, and when he came into the kitchen all Kayla could do was smile when he walked up behind her at the stove and wrapped his arms around her waist. A soft kiss on the back of her neck sent a chill down her spine, and the feeling of his dick against her ass made it kind of hard to focus on his pancakes. "You better stop before you get ya'self in trouble!" she warned, giving him a flirtatious smile.

Qua had to admit to himself that Kayla did things last night that no other woman had ever done to him before. Her insides were so wet and tight that it made him cum within the first ten strokes of round one. He was damn near done from that, but he quickly rallied back for another round.

It was round two that put Kayla back in her place as he did things to her that she'd never experienced before in her life. Qua made love to her and explored every part of her body with the most gentle of touches. He gave her passion, pleasure and a hint of pain. Her body gave into his every command, giving him everything she had. Sometimes sex can change everything about a relationship, for either the good or the bad. But after last night it seemed to bring Kayla and Qua only closer.

Agent Flint walked alongside the Hudson River, watching the scuba divers pull a body out of the water. JahJah's body had finally turned up a couple days later. Mitch didn't even give the Milano's a chance to give her a proper burial.

When the divers got to shore and zipped down the body bag, Flint knew exactly who it was at first glance. He still couldn't understand how body after body from the Milano Family kept turning up. This wasn't just any old local gang or clique this was the Mafia.

"So, what you think?" Agent Parker asked Flint as they looked down at the body.

"I don't know, but it seems like we should be trying to protect the Milano's instead of trying to put them in jail," Flint said, walking off and lighting the cigarette he had in his mouth.

Valentina told Semaj about the poachers, and if she ever caught one trying to steal any plants from her field, she should just kill them on the spot. Every time a new coca field gets started, that is when they come out. They try to steal as much coke as they can, then sell it to the lower level drug dealers of Columbia. If they steal enough, it could be very profitable for them. They are like the hyenas of the drug world. They would risk their lives to steal anything.

Semaj got down on the ground and crawled military style in her field. She and Vikingo had been watching the field ever since a patch of plants was taken the night before. Semaj wanted to make an example out of the thief so this problem wouldn't happen again anytime soon.

In the distance she could see a poacher about a half mile away with a bag around his neck and stuffing plants into it. Vikingo was right behind her, keeping his eyes on the poacher and on Semaj. The poacher wasn't even aware that he was being watched, and like a gazelle in lion territory, he was being stalked.

They got as close as they possibly could get without being seen, and then in Semaj's moment of truth. She grabbed the large AK-47 with both hands, looked back at Vikingo with a smile on her face, and then took off running. She waited a moment before firing a shot, because the poacher still didn't see her. But when he did, he took off running. Semaj let the AK go, firing at him as she ran towards him. This was the first time she'd ever fired a gun this big, and it was a little difficult running and shooting at the same time.

Vikingo just stood up and started walking, because he knew from experience that she had jumped the gun and wouldn't be able to catch the poacher.

She kept chasing him though, popping off multiple shots at the runner. Bullets kicked up dirt right behind his feet, but she just couldn't keep up, especially toting a gun that was almost as tall as she was. She stopped and watched as the poacher ran off the field. She was tired as hell and knelt down to try and catch her breath.

"Ha-ha-ha!" Vikingo laughed as he walked up to where she was. "You look like you're about to fall out," he said, kneeling down beside her.

"I could have had him if you would have helped me!" she barked back. "Why didn't you help me?"

"It wouldn't have mattered if I helped you or not. The poacher is too fast. You have to get a lot closer if you wanna catch one of them."

"Why didn't you tell me that?" she asked, still trying to catch her breath.

"I really needed a good laugh!"

She stood up and playfully hit Vikingo in his chest. They had gotten close over the past few weeks, and their friendship was growing day by day. Sometimes Semaj would flirt with him but he seemed reluctant to flirt back. But that didn't stop her from lusting after him. Semaj was actually surprised that she was so attracted to a Columbian. She always looked at the black man as the dominant race, and was attracted to them the most. But

Vikingo was also strong in many ways as a black man was, and she saw that the only difference between the two was that the Columbian men treated their women differently. They literally worshipped the ground they walked on, and waited on them hand and foot. In Semaj's experience with some black man, it seemed that once they put it down on you in the bed it then became the woman's obligation to cater to the man.

Semaj and Vikingo stood there laughing and joking about the poacher. There was a physical attraction they both shared for each other, and it was times like these when it became difficult for them to resist one another. Today, standing in the middle of the coca field with nobody else around, they took in the quiet, peaceful, and oddly romantic scenery. Vikingo looked into her eyes and didn't say a word. He stepped in put his hand on her waist and kissed her. This took Semaj by surprise, but she put up no resistance, pressing her soft full lips up against his.

He took the AK from off her shoulder, lifted her off her feet and placed her gently onto a small patch of grass. He rubbed his fingers through her hair, pushed it out of the way, and kissed the scar on the side of her face. This let her know that she was still beautiful. If Semaj didn't know any better, she would have thought that he was in love with her from the way he looked her in the eyes. It was exciting and captivating, and before Semaj knew it, he was taking off his shirt. She didn't protest, but rather sat up enough to kiss his ripped chest. It had been so long since she had sex and she welcomed feeling all of him inside of her.

He laid her down on her back, reached for her cargo pants and pulled them off, while she took off her tank top. He stood up and unbuckled his jeans, dropped them to the ground, knelt back down and got on top of Semaj. He kissed her lips and then lightly guided his hands down the center of her stomach. He left a warm trail of kisses all the way down to her belly.

Semaj could hardly control herself, anticipating him tasting her sweetness. When his mouth finally made it down bellow, she jumped at the touch of his lips kissing her clit. She put her hand on the back of his head and rubbed her hand through his silky hair. The warmth of his mouth felt incredible His head swayed from left to right and his tongue felt like it was searching for her G-spot the way he slid it inside of her. She grabbed her breast and pinched her nipple with her thumb and index finger. It wasn't long until she could feel the tingling sensation at the bottom of her stomach, indicating that she was about to cum. She inhaled deeply and exhaled with a moan. Her body went into convolutions, shaking uncontrollably as she reached her orgasm. She squeezed Vikingo's head in between her legs. Her juices splashed all over his chin and she jerked like she was having a seizure while trying to push his head away.

His tongue led another warm trail back up the center of her stomach, all the way back to her mouth. At the same time and without even touching it, his dick slid right inside of her. She had a shocked look on her face as his massive tool entered and filled her up inside. Just when she thought it was all the way in, he pushed more of it inside of her. She flinched from the tension and grabbed onto his back, biting down on his shoulder from the pain that turned into pleasure. His stroke was long, slow, strong and deep, making her call out his name. "Vikingo," she whispered in his ear and kissed the side of his face softly. "It feels so good!" she moaned, feeling him dig his way inside of her.

Feeling her walls collapsing on his dick, Vikingo felt himself ready to cum. He never had pussy so wet before. He could feel Semaj's body shake, and the more it shook the wetter it got.

"I'm Cumming!" she whispered in his ear. "Don't stop! Go deeper!" she cried, breathing heavily in his ear.

Vikingo too was at that point, and sped up his strokes as he chased his orgasm. It was too good. He wanted to, but he couldn't pull out. He released his warm cum deep inside of her while yelling out her name from pleasure. "Semaj! Oh, Semaj!" he yelled, before placing his tongue into her mouth.

They both lay there in disbelief as to how they'd let it get this far. The sexual tension had built up so much that it only took Semaj running through a coca field with an AK to bring things to a head. They lay in the coca field marinating in each other's fluids and enjoying each other's comfort.

Vikingo had given Semaj everything she needed, and then some, at a time when she felt at her lowest, mentally and physically. All of the sudden in the middle of relaxing, Qua came into her thoughts.

Jeramie sat in the back room of the restaurant he owned, counting the money he was going to let Quasim use at the 16 Tent meeting, when the sound of a commotion in the dining area caught his attention. He looked at the security monitors and saw dread heads with guns, laying down the customers. He immediately pushed all the cash into a trash bag and grabbed a shotgun from out of his locker. He didn't know the reason they were there, and he really didn't care. Whoever it was, they were looking for trouble in the wrong establishment, especially if they were trying to rob it.

Jeramie continued staring at the monitor and waited for the right time to bust out of the door and start shooting. There was a lot of yelling going on, but nothing was happening, that is until Chazz came from behind the register and started firing at the Jamaicans. His first bullet pretty much knocked a couple dreads out of one of the Jamaican's head, which caused him to slump over a table.

The second Jake turned and shot back at Chazz, forcing him to run back behind the counter. When one Jamaican dropped another came crashing through the door. Bullets were flying in the restaurant, most of which were in Chazz's direction.

Jeramie saw an opportunity and took it. He left the back room and unleashed the 12-gauge pump rapidly. Blue fire spit out of the pump, and just the sound of it alone made the two Jakes that were left get low to the ground. As he walked up on the two of them, he just so happened to glance out the window. He turned around and took cover just in time to avoid the two armed men outside of the window, shooting in.

Bullets broke through the glass, hitting everything in the restaurant.

Chazz wasn't quick enough to get out of the way, and neither was one of the Jamaicans. They both got hit with multiple rounds to their bodies. Jeramie watched as his friend's body fell to the floor. He was dead before his face touched the carpet.

Jeramie jumped up in the midst of the shooting and released a few more rounds from the pump as he backed into his office. He entered in and slammed the door behind him, tossed the pump to the floor and grabbed a .9mm from his desk drawer. He looked into the monitor and could see the armed Jamaicans pouring into the restaurant. There was no way he was going to win the gun battle, so his only option was to get out through the back door.

He grabbed the trash bag full of money and headed down the little hallway that led to the loading dock. The sound of gunfire at his office door prompted him to move a little faster so he picked up his to a jog.

Once he got to the back door and opened it, his face

ran right into a two by four piece of lumber that Ox had swung at him. The blow busted his face wide open, knocked most of his front teeth out, broke his nose and knocked him out cold.

Ox stood over him and looked down with fury in his eyes. He didn't just want to kill Jeramie, he wanted him to die by torture. Rude-Boy was his heart…his only son, and Jeramie had taken that away from him. The price he had to pay for that was going to be heavy. He dragged his unconscious body to the van he had waiting, tossed him in the back and pulled off.

Valentina knocked on Semaj's door and peeked in to see if she was there. The sound of the shower running in the bathroom confirmed that she was. She waited, taking a seat on her bed. When Semaj came out the shower she was a little startled, walking into her bedroom and seeing Valentina sitting on her bed. "Hey, Valentina," she said, and walked over to the mirror.

"If you ever call me Valentina again, I'ma get a switch and beat ya ass with it!" she joked. "From now on, you call me Grandma, Grandmother, or any other name that symbolizes who I am to you. Are we clear?" she asked with a stern look on her face.

"Yes, Grandma," Semaj responded with a smile.

"Now, I want you to accompany Jorge to the 16 Tent

meeting in Hawaii in a couple of days. Let me know how your field is doing and how much cocaine it has produced so far."

"What happened to you? Why aren't you going to the meeting?" Semaj asked her. She knew that there were only two people per family allowed at the table.

"One thing you're going to learn is that I'm the boss of this family, and whatever I say goes, no questions asked. One day you'll be a boss like me and you will know exactly what I'm talking about. Now, do what I told you and get back to me tonight," she said, and got up to leave. "Oh, and Vikingo is a nice boy. I like him," she said before she left.

Semaj just sat down on her bed and smiled. She was thinking about representing the Espriella Family at the 16 Tent meeting. This was big. Shit, it was huge.

With the fully grown plants Valentina provided for her to get her field started, she had enough to produce about six or seven tons within a couple days. Given a little more time, that number could increase dramatically. But for now this was what she was working with. It might have been a small number to Valentina, but it was a lot for Semaj who never dealt anything over four tons in her life. *Damn, the pressure is on!* Semaj thought to herself as she rubbed lotion on her body and got ready for dinner with Vikingo. "Damn, the pressure is on!" she said again, shaking her head.

Chapter 14

"Are you sure it was Murda Mitch?" Bonjo asked LuLu, who was sitting on the couch in the living room while Marcela stitched her arm up.

"I think I'd know Murda Mitch if I saw him!" she snapped back with an attitude. "I shot him, but he had a vest on. Damn! I can't believe dat mufucka still alive!"

Bonjo couldn't believe it either. Why wouldn't Gio tell him anything so important before he died? Mitch was a maniac, and Bonjo also knew what he was hittin' for when it came down to his murder game. Bonjo had to sit and think. He wondered why Mitch would go so hard on the family. Then, a light bulb turned on in his head when he thought about Semaj. What man wouldn't go hard for his seed? "He thinks Semaj is dead, and he probably thinks we had something to do with it!" Bonjo said, staring off in deep thought.

"Why would he think we killed Semaj?" Emilia asked with a curious look on her face.

"Before Mitch went missing, his daughter was with us,

and now that he's back she's dead. If I was him I wouldn't care whether the Milano Family killed her or didn't. I would murder everyone who had taken responsibility for her wellbeing. With daughters, fathers can be ruthless, and you wouldn't believe the things a man would do if he thought you killed his only child," Bonjo said breaking it down in the simplest terms he could.

The girls may not have understood what Bonjo was saying, but he knew exactly what needed to be done. He was going to have to find Mitch and kill him before he annihilated the entire Milano Family. But first he had to get him to show his face, something that was a suicide mission in itself. The one thing about Bonjo was that for his family, he was willing to sacrifice his life so that the Milano name could live on.

The plane touched down on American soil and Sosa was relieved that she had Nyala with her. There was still a DNA test ahead, but Sosa had a motherly instinct that Nyala was her daughter.

The first thing she did was take her daughter shopping. There was no time to pack any of her clothes, and frankly she wouldn't have wanted to. She wanted to leave everything behind in Jamaica and start Nyala's life over completely with a mother who was going to love and protect her with every breath she took.

They had fun all day running around the mall and

hitting every store Nyala pointed her little finger at. Nyala ran around so much that she ended up falling asleep on Sosa's lap in the food court. It was at that moment when she was asleep that Sosa realized that her entire life was about to change. She was a mother again, and she was enjoying every second of it.

When Sosa and Nyala finally walked through the front door of the Milano house, everyone's jaw dropped. They hadn't heard from Sosa in weeks, and for that they all thought that she was dead. To see her alive was a joy, but that joy quickly turned into concern when they saw the little girl standing beside her.

"Who is that?" LuLu asked when she saw the little girl from the parade. She had a clue as to who she was, but she wanted it hear what Sosa had to say.

"I know that ain't who I think it is!" Marcela snapped, also remembering the little girl from Jamaica.

Everyone in the room got quiet, waiting to hear the answer. Nyala got a little scared of the girls and hid behind her mother's leg where she knew that she would be well protected.

"You went to Jamaica and took that little girl!" Emilia exclaimed after Sosa still didn't answer. "I know that ain't Ox's kid!"

"Ox's kid?" Bonjo jumped up and walked over to Sosa. "Are you out ya fucking mind going over there and kidnapping his little girl?" he shouted at Sosa as he thought about what he just told the other sisters about how unpredictable men could be about their daughters.

"Fuck that! We got to kill her and bury her ass in the woods some got-damn where!" LuLu said, getting up from her seat.

Sosa reached in her back pocket and grabbed the .38 snub nose she had gotten the minute she got into the city and placed it at her thigh. LuLu and Bonjo backed away, thinking that she must have been out of her mind. But she wasn't out of her mind. She was thinking about where she should begin with how this little girl ended up being her daughter. "This is my daughter," she said, shocking the hell out of everybody. "And for starters, her name is Nyala."

"She's ya what!" Bonjo asked, scratching his head.

"Why does every fuckin' body keep pulling guns out on me!" LuLu complained when Sosa pulled out hers.

"It's ya mouth. Learn how to control it," Sosa snapped before putting the gun back in her back pocket. It took a while, but Sosa broke down the entire story about her, Ox and her father. She told them about going over to Jamaica by herself and why she didn't tell anybody about it.

It all made sense, and there was nothing anybody could do but respect her move. At the same time she wasn't going to let nobody hurt her child, and after hearing what she said, Bonjo understood her over protectiveness. Emilia had heard enough. If Sosa said this was her seed, then that's what it was point blank. She walked over to the little girl and knelt down in front of her. "My name is Auntie Em. You wanna come get some juice with me?"

she asked Nyala and held her hand out.

Nyala looked at her mom, the woman who went through hell and back to get her. She wasn't going to move or trust anybody unless she approved of it. Sosa knelt down in front of Nyala and said to her, "This is your family now. Nobody here will ever hurt you, baby girl. I promise."

"Not even that big ol' monster over there?" she smiled while pointing at LuLu who had walked over and knelt down in front of her too.

It was Marcela who rushed over and scooped little Nyala up and ran off into the kitchen with her. LuLu and Emilia chased after them, wanting to get to know their niece. Bonjo stayed behind. There was so much he had to tell Sosa since she'd been gone. She wasn't aware of Ortiz's or JahJah's deaths. He had to bring her up to speed about everything that was going on. She had no idea what she'd just walked into. But first, he wanted to deal with the issue at hand. "You know Ox is going to come for his daughter," he said.

"Yeah, I know. I'm expecting him to," Sosa responded, knowing it was about to go down.

"Wake up, pussy boy!" Ox said, and threw a bag of salt in Jeramie's bloody face.

The salt burned every exposed and open wound on

Jeramie's face. He woke up in the worst kind of pain. Cracking his eye, he could see a dread headed man looking down on him with an ax in his hand. The one thing about Jeramie was that he wasn't afraid of shit. What Ox had planned for him was nothing to him. He was raised by people that took honor in dying by torture. But if he was going down, he surely wasn't going alone. "Who sent you? Was it da nigga, Quasim?" he asked before spitting the blood in his mouth onto the floor.

"You don't worry 'bout dat boy. I gonna kill you ten times!" Ox responded with a crazed look in his eyes. "You kill me boy! Me only boy! Ox gonna make you pay!"

"Fuck is you talking about?" Jeramie asked. He didn't know what Ox was ranting about.

Ox punched him across the jaw, knocking blood out of his mouth. Jeramie took the punch and then started smiling. It was like an insult to Ox, but Ox smiled with him.

"Let me...let me guess. Rude-Boy must be ya people," Jeramie got out before spitting out another glob of blood.

Hearing his name coming from Jeramie only made Ox even angrier. He took the back of the ax and crushed Jeramie's hand that was tied to the chair.

Not only did Jeramie smile, but this time he also laughed and spit blood onto Ox's shoe. "He's playin' you real good. You think I killed Rude-Boy? Ask yourself this...Ox. Yeeaahh! I know who you are now!" he said, eyeing Ox who looked surprised that he knew his name. "Answer the million dollar question, Ox. Why...why would I kill Rude-Boy? I never had a reason to. But ya boy Qua, he got all the reasons in the world," he said, leaning back in the chair.

Ox always felt that something was wrong with Qua. He always knew how to talk fast and sound convincing when he lied. What was the reason that Jeramie had to kill Rude-Boy? There was none. Up until he had met Qua, he didn't even know who Rude-Boy was. This made Ox want to get to the bottom of things. "Tell me what ya know, boy, and I'll t'ink 'bout letting you live," Ox said, and squatted down in front of Jeramie.

Jeramie laughed at the suggestion. He knew beyond a shadow of a doubt that this basement was his final resting place. He also knew that Qua put all this together. It sounded like something he would do if he were in Qua's shoes. Ox wasn't going to let him go, but before he was killed, he was going to make sure that Qua got murdered too for setting him up. He didn't know why Qua did it, but he knew for sure that he was the one that got him in this predicament. "Qua killed Rude-Boy. He's taking over London and he simply got rid of the competition," Jeramie told Ox before laughing in his face.

What he said sounded more believable than anything Qua had told him up until this point. Ox stood up after he had heard enough and circled the chair with the ax in his hand. Jeramie watched him until he couldn't see Ox any more. He gripped the chair bracing for an impact. Ox cocked the ax way above his head, and then brought it down with all his strength. The ax hacked into Jeramie's head, almost cutting in half. It opened up like a cantaloupe and killed Jeramie instantly.

Ox left the basement leaving the ax stuck in Jeramie's head. He didn't even enjoy killing him. It was Qua whom he wanted now, and that's where he was on his way to.

Paris looked at the aftermath from the shootout the other night. She watched as a few guards went through the rubble left behind from the house catching on fire. Her arm was starting to ache from the deep graze she sustained during the shootout, but the minor pain she was feeling was nothing compared to what Ox was going to do to her for letting his daughter get kidnapped right from under her nose.

She looked down at her cell phone but did not want to call him. She didn't want to be the one to break the news to him, but she really didn't have any other choice. Nobody from his camp wanted to do it, not even the head of his security. Ox was definitely the type to kill the messenger, but somebody had to tell him, so she dialed his number. She was hoping that he wouldn't pick up the phone, but he did on the third ring.

"Yo, g'won," he answered as he drove down the highway on his way to meet up with Qua.

"Hey, baby," she said hesitantly, not knowing how to break the news to him. "We got a problem out here.

Something happened, and I think you need to come home."

"Wha ya talking 'bout?" he shot back after hearing the distress in her voice.

"Somebody came in and took Nyala."

It got real quiet on the phone, and Ox didn't know if he had heard her right. "Wha ya say, girl?" he asked, wanting her to repeat herself.

She didn't want to. The first time was hard enough, and now she had to say it again. "Somebody came here and took Nyala. She's gone, Ox. The fucking Milano sisters came through here," she said, thinking that it had to be all of them who did all this damage. "Hello? Hello?" she yelled into a dead phone. "Shit!" she mumbled after seeing that Ox wasn't on the phone any longer.

Ox looked up at the highway signs and turned off at the next exit. His plan for killing Qua had to be postponed until further notice. His passion for murder was directed to another place. Qua wasn't that hard to find, and after he took care of everyone that was a part of his daughter's kidnapping, he would get right back to business with Qua. Right now, his destination was home, and he needed to get there pronto.

Since arriving in Miami it only tempted Semaj to want to vacation there for a few days. The weather was beautiful and there were more than enough activities to do in one day. Everything around you seemed like non-stop action.

She walked onto the small baseball field accompanied by heavily armed guards that stood behind her. She looked like a straight New Yorker. She had on blue jeans, a wife beater, a pair of air Max's and carried a Louis Vuitton bag.

Haitian Frank was standing alone at the pitcher's mound waiting for her. He didn't need security next to him, but he did have shooters at close range just in case things got out of hand. It shouldn't get that far because they were only there to discuss prices and not make the actual transaction.

"Semaj," she introduced herself, sticking out her hand for a shake.

"Frank," he responded, extending his hand. "Let's walk and talk," he suggested, wanting to get away from the rest of the ears. Semaj obliged and waved her guards off so they wouldn't follow them as they walked away. The guards stood by with watchful eyes as she walked off with Frank.

Frank looked kind of surprised that the pretty young woman standing before him was ready to discuss cocaine prices. Although he had never seen Valentina, he got the word of what she looked like and this definitely wasn't her. He did realize that Semaj had to be somebody of importance though. "Is Semaj your real name, or…"

"Look, Frank. I'ma get straight down to business," she said, cutting him off from trying to make small talk. "I'm here to negotiate the prices, and that's all. Now, I understand that you are interested in finding a new connect."

He couldn't do anything but respect her G as a woman. In fact, he liked it and was eager to do business with her. He felt like he didn't have to worry about any games being played with the product or with his money.

Haitian Frank pretty much ran Miami and most of the surrounding cities. His only problem was that Ox's cocaine wasn't worth shit. It was some high price bullshit that really wasn't worth buying. It had been tapped a couple times before it even got to him, and although the Ox was from Jamaica, Frank knew that there was better coke out there. One thing was for certain is that Frank didn't give a fuck who Ox was. If a better product came along he was jumping ship ASAP.

"I'm looking to buy around five hundred kilos of pure cocaine. I need that amount delivered probably twice a month," Frank put out there. "I'm looking to get it at the best price as well," he added.

"If you don't mind me asking, how much were you paying for a brick before, not that it matters?" Semaj asked.

"Right now I'm paying twelve thousand a brick and the coke is pretty average. If you can top that, then we can do business. If not, then it was nice meeting you," he shot back with a straight face.

Semaj smiled. She knew that she had this deal in the bag. Twelve thousand a brick was way too much, especially when you were buying a half-ton or better a month. Whoever he was buying from was robbing him blind. "Well, I'm willing to go as low as eight thousand a brick as long as you can guarantee buying a ton a month. My cocaine is grade-A product straight from the coca field. You can hit it five or six times and it will still be the best cocaine in Florida, hands down. I will have it delivered wherever you want upon demand, and those services will be free of charge too."

Frank couldn't believe his ears at the prices and the delivery service. He just nodded his head in approval, trying to keep his cool. He had to play gangsta, but on the inside he was like a kid in a candy store. This was the kind of connect he'd been looking for ever since he'd been in the drug game. It was hard trying to find someone who did business the right way, and there was no question as to whether or not he was jumping on board with Semaj. It was only a matter of how fast she could get it to him.

Before the meeting was concluded, his first shipment of the pearly-white was due to be delivered ASAP.

Semaj walked off the baseball field and headed back to the car where Jorge was waiting for her. He didn't want to be all over her back and butting in during the deal so he just let her do her thing solo. This was really only a test just to see where she was at.

"So?" Jorge asked, looking out of the window when

Semaj got into the car.

"So, he wants a ton delivered by tomorrow. Here's the time and location," she said and passed him a small piece of paper.

He looked at Semaj and smiled. Not only did she get Frank as a customer, she managed to get him to buy a ton of cocaine on his first shot. Semaj had a natural instinct to sell cocaine, and Jorge could see every bit of his sister in her. It wouldn't be much longer until she was ready.

Chapter 15

Hawaii Conference

Semaj was anxious to see who else was going to show up from the Milano Family at the meeting. She hadn't seen anybody from that side of her family since Gio's funeral, where she was pretty much ostracized.

She was surprised when she walked into the meeting and saw everyone from the other families sitting there and talking and joking as usual. She felt like she had finally made it this time as she stood in for Valentina. Her family was much bigger and more important than the Milano Family. The Espriella Family was playing with a lot more money than pretty much everybody sitting at the table.

"Nikolai, Marko, Mr. Wong, Mr. and Mrs. Naoroji…" she acknowledged everyone at the table.

When she took a seat in Valentina's place they all looked at each other and wondered whether she was being rude, or just made an honest mistake.

Jorge entered the tent and took a seat next to her with a smile on his face.

"Where's Valentina?" Nikolai asked with a confused look on his face.

Everyone sat up in anticipation waiting for an answer to the question. But just before Jorge was about to answer, Bonjo and Emilia walked into the tent and apologized for their lateness.

What seemed like a lifetime ago, Semaj finally laid her eyes on the Milano Family, or at least what was left of them. Emilia looked at Semaj with confusion and wondered what she was doing there. Bonjo thought the same thing while nodding in her direction to acknowledge her.

They all turned to look at Bonjo and Emilia, and wondered where Ortiz was. They had no idea that he was dead, nor did they know that Bonjo was taking over as the boss of the Milano Family.

Quiet whispers began throughout the tent, and things got even more confusing for some when Quasim stepped under the tent, dressed to impress. He wore a Zilli wool and silk suit, a Prada shirt and a pair of Hermes shoes. His hair was styled in a Caesar cut, and they could the smell the scent of Clive Christian. He came in and sat in the Abbott's seat all by himself, claiming London, England. The whispers continued until Bonjo called for the meeting to start.

Semaj and Quasim hadn't seen each other in what felt like forever. They locked eyes and for that moment they looked at each other as if they were the only two people in the room. *He looks so fuckin' good sitting there,*

Semaj thought to herself. Qua gave her a casual piece sign and then looked away to hear what Bonjo had to say.

"I guess this is going to be an interesting meeting," Bonjo said, standing at the head of the table. "Now, before we get started, let me go around the room and let everyone introduce themselves, starting with you," he said, pointing to Quasim.

"I'm Quasim. The Abbott family is dead, so I stepped up for London. You can call my organization the 'London Family' if that makes things more convenient," he said as he looked around the room, making eye contact with every single person.

"Nikolai," Nikolai said with a wave of his fingers.

"Wong Won," Won announced, also waving his hand.

"Naoroji Family," Ezra announced for Africa.

When it got around to Semaj, they were waiting to hear what she was going to say. She stood up, pressing her knuckles on the table. "I recently found out that my grandmother is Maria Valentina Espriella. I am here on her behalf. My name is Semaj Espriella, and all business coming from Columbia will come through me from now on," she said with a firm voice and looking each and every one of them in the eye before retaking her seat.

"I knew there was something about that girl!" Nikolai whispered to Won.

The room got a little noisy. It was as if everyone had something to say about the changes that were happening.

Qua looked at Semaj, impressed with the way she was tossing around her authority. She was representing the part well too, sitting there in a three-piece Ermenegildo Zegna pants suit, a Kiton eyelet shirt and a pair of Louis Vuitton leather pumps. Her hair was pulled back in a ponytail, showing off her battle scars. He couldn't take his eyes off of her.

Bonjo couldn't believe that Semaj was claiming another family's name, and now was his key supplier of cocaine. She was pretty much the boss, and it made it difficult to go on with the meeting, knowing he was going to have to ask her for a favor.

"I'm Bonjo Milano. Ortiz is dead and I'm now the head of the Milano Family," he said carrying the weight of his family's stress all over his face.

The room suddenly got quiet and nobody said a word after hearing that he was the Milano Family boss. It wasn't that the other families didn't like him; they just felt that he wasn't ready for that type of responsibility. But they had no say in the matter. Each family decided how the control got passed down.

"Well, I'm here to buy 500 kilos," Qua said, looking around the room.

Everybody looked at Semaj, who sat there like the boss that she was.

"So, are the prices the same or have things changed?" Bonjo asked, wanting clarity for himself.

"I'm in a position to sell my kilos at six-thousand five-hundred for anyone who buys two tons or better at one time; and seven thousand a kilo for anyone who buys one ton or better. Anything less than a ton will be sold for seventy-five-hundred a kilo. So, the more you buy, the cheaper it gets. Delivery will cost depending on the location, and I guarantee that every delivery will be successful, no ifs ands or buts about it," she said, speaking as though she'd been there before.

The meeting continued, and all families established their product and the prices behind it. Nikolai wanted to talk about something other than drugs, and Won agreed with Nikolai about his concerns.

"What direction is the Milano Family going in? I mean, it seems like you can't handle your problems with the Jamaicans, and you don't want anybody's help," Nikolai said and took a puff of his cigar. "Should we expect to see you here at the next meeting?" he questioned with all honesty.

"I'm glad you asked that, Nikolai, because I don't think the Espriella Family is willing to continue doing business with the Milano's until their problem with the Jamaicans is handled," Semaj stated, looking at Bonjo.

Bonjo sat there biting his lower lip in frustration. He couldn't believe that Semaj was refusing to do business with him, because she had the same problems when she was with the Milano Family. He felt like she was using her newfound status to get back at the family because they banished her. He was hot on the inside, especially because it wasn't just the Jamaicans that they had a problem with. "I wanna assure everybody at this table that this problem will be resolved in…"

"Well, until you get ya problem resolved we have to

put a stop to all business until further notice," Semaj said, rudely cutting him off.

Bonjo bit his tongue. He wanted to say something disrespectful to her, but he had to at least act like a boss while he was in the presence of a few important ones. He simply asked if anybody else had any other concerns before the meeting was over, and when everybody was satisfied, he adjourned the meeting for the day.

"Fuck you, Semaj!" Bonjo said as he walked up to her while she was talking to Qua after the meeting. He was fed up with her superior attitude. During the entire meeting she'd been talking down to him like he was some shit at the bottom of her shoe. "You wanna know something? Ya father shot LuLu, killed my wife, and he killed Ortiz! And when I find him I swear by the name of this family, I'ma put a bullet in between his eyes!"

Semaj wasn't sure if she had heard Bonjo right. "What did you say about my father?" she asked calmly.

"You heard what I said!" he shot back, looking her dead in the eyes. "He's dead!" he said, and turned to walk away.

Semaj grabbed his arm. "Don't take my humbleness and this suit as a sign of weakness, Uncle Jo. I'm not the same little girl y'all kicked out of the family," she mumbled so that the rest of the families that were still in the tent couldn't hear her. "If my father is still alive…"

"So you mean to tell me that Murda Mitch is still alive?" Qua asked, looking at Semaj but waiting for Bonjo to answer.

"Yeah, but not for long," he answered, and snatched his arm away from Semaj then stormed out from under the tent.

Qua didn't say another word either. He just simply buttoned his suit, dusted his jacket off and walked off. Without a doubt, he was on his way to New York to holla at Mitch. He didn't care how Semaj would feel or the repercussions that may come with it. He was going to kill Mitch for killing his father, and there was nothing anybody could say to convince him otherwise.

As Semaj watched everybody walk quickly back to their cars, she couldn't help but notice the tall, exotic looking woman that was waiting for Qua. She didn't have to wonder who she was, as Qua kissed her right before getting into the car. It was clear that part of her life was done and over with but she still wasn't ready to let go. Her and Qua had been through so much together and the love they shared was still there at least on her end and she believed it did for Qua too. He did save her life after all. She knew he must've felt some kinda way that after the Ox incident she basically vanished and cut off contact with him. But for Semaj it was something she had to do in order to get her mind right and become the Boss that she felt she was born to be. Handling business was her top priority.

There was one major obstacle that now stood in the way of a reconciliation even if she was willing to fight to get Qua back…her father. Qua was determined to make her dad pay for murdering his father and Semaj couldn't allow that. Family came first and if Qua was threatening to kill Murda Mitch then he mind as well be pointing the gun at her because now that Semaj knew her father was alive she was going to do everything possible to keep it that way.

"Is everything alright?" Jorge asked her.

"Yeah, everything's good. I just got to go to New York for a few days. Tell my grandmother I had to take care of something and I'll call and talk to her about it later," she said, and left the tent.

Ox looked out of the small window as the plane flew over his house before landing. He could see that the fire had leveled the entire house and there was nothing left but burnt rubble. He clenched his teeth at the sight of it and had already planned to kill many, many people behind this act of war.

Once on the ground, he drove up to what was his house. He looked around at all the damage in disbelief. He was mad as hell that his security let it go down like that. His people kept trying to come up to him and tell him what happened, but he waved them off. He didn't want to hear a single word they had to say. The only person he asked for was Paris, but she had taken a commercial flight the first thing in the morning, back to New York. She told one of the guards that she was going to try and get Nyala back.

Ox got back in his car, and without saying a word his driver already knew that he was headed back to the airport. New York was his destination.

Chapter 16

"Good morning, Your Honor. In light of the evidence we were able to obtain throughout the course of the past several months, the FBI is asking Your Honor for warrants to search properties owned by the Milano Family," Agent Flint said, standing in front of the bench.

"What kind of evidence do you have? Because you know I just can't give out warrants without probable cause," the judge replied, interlocking his fingers with anticipation of hearing something good for a change.

Agent Flint gave the judge the entire spiel on everything they had against the Milano Family. They had bought drugs from people within the organization, and had hours of wiretaps linking almost everybody in the family to a drug deal of some kind. Video surveillance showed that they were armed every time they left the house. He told the judge about multiple shootings that involved members of the family, and he even mentioned the hit that was placed on the family.

Flint really did his homework on the Milano clan, and by the end of the day it was nothing for him to obtain the warrants that he requested. It was the physical evidence that was needed to seal the case, and that's what the warrants were for.

Flint walked out of the Federal Building with the warrant signed by the judge. It was going to take a tactical procedure to hit all the Milano's establishments simultaneously. That would be his only chance at finding any physical evidence, and at this stage in the investigation he didn't want to blow it. He wasn't even going to tell SWAT and the search team that he had a warrant for fear that it might be leaked to the family. If that ever happened, Flint could kiss his case goodbye.

Semaj had been in the city for an entire day now and she still couldn't find Murda Mitch. She'd looked everywhere she thought he could possibly be hiding out, but to no avail. She did get a chance to talk to Sosa who had set up a lunch date with her and the baby. Sosa was probably the only one in the Milano Family that didn't hate her. She understood everything that Semaj had gone through, especially with the loss of her son. The bond that they had built was stronger than the one either of them had with anyone in their families.

Semaj walked into the hospital where she was supposed to meet Sosa and Nyala. Vikingo and two other guards accompanied her per the request of Valentina.

Semaj wasn't to go anywhere by herself under any circumstances, not even for lunch with a close relative.

Sosa was at the hospital taking a DNA test just to have proof that Nyala was her daughter. When Semaj got to the room she could see Sosa and the little girl sitting on a hospital bed, laughing and playing with some toys. She almost cried at the sight of how happy Sosa looked playing with her seed. She seemed to be at peace.

"Hey!" Semaj said, as she entered the room with her arms open wide for a hug. "Is this my niece?" she smiled and lightly pinched Nyala's chubby cheeks.

Sosa smiled at Semaj's introduction, but quickly noticed the men standing outside of the room. She looked at Semaj and could see a big change in her. The first thing she noticed was the thick scar running down the side of her face, and then she took a good look at her. She wasn't the little princess that Gio used to baby all the time. She looked all grown up, and from the way she was heavily guarded she looked like a boss again.

"Come here, girl!" Semaj said and hugged and kissed Sosa. "So this is ya seed, huh?" she asked, putting her hand on the top of Nyala's head. "This little girl looks just like you." She kissed Nyala's forehead.

"Yeah, this is my seed. I took a test today to be safe, but I know in my heart this is my baby girl."

"So, did you hear anything from you know who?" Semaj asked without having to mention Ox's name.

"Girl, I tore that nigga's shit up!" Sosa grinned and flipped open her cell phone to show Semaj a couple pictures she took of the fire being put out as she flew over it in the plane.

Semaj didn't expect anything less from Sosa. She went hard for her seed. She could only imagine what else she did when she was in Jamaica.

"I know he's on his way, but I really don't give a fuck. He's probably already here, thinking of some kind of master plan to kill me and take my seed back. But let me tell you this, Maj. I'ma send that nigga back to Jamaica in a body bag if he comes here tryin' to fuck wit' this here, ya feel me?" she said with a sincere look in her eyes.

Just then the doctor came into the room with some papers in his hand. He wasn't going to say anything with Semaj in the room, but Sosa quickly let him know that she was her family and that it was cool to say what the results were.

It was to no surprise the DNA test proved that without a doubt Nyala was Sosa's daughter. Even still, it brought tears to Sosa's eyes as she looked down at her only child. Ox was going to have to pry her out of Sosa's dead hand if he wanted her back, which was the one thing he wouldn't have a problem doing.

Bonjo sat in the back of the car talking to Marcela about what had happened at the 16 Tent meeting, and how more than likely they would have to find a new drug supplier within the United States until things got situated.

Marcela was shocked to hear that Semaj was now a part of the Espriella Family, and how Gio had gone all this time without telling anybody the truth about Kasey and Semaj. Nevertheless, business had to go on. Despite everything that had went down up until now, the Milano's was still the most dominant family on the East Coast. In order for them to be able to maintain that status they would have to keep supplying cocaine on demand.

"So who's going to be the new connect?" Marcela asked, turning the headrest TV on.

"I'm going down to Mexico in a couple days. I got an old friend there that I use to do business with back in the day. Don't worry about the new supplier. Just make sure we keep moving the rest of the work we got left on the streets. By then we should have some grade-A cocaine straight from across the border," Bonjo said as he watched the news on the TV. "Have you heard anything about Mitch yet?" he asked, thinking of how he had become a major problem as of late as well.

"LuLu is on his head. She said something about seeing him at a bar last night. I haven't seen her since."

"Yeah? The quicker we get that crazy mufucka off the streets, the better."

The driver rolled down the partition told them that they had to stop for gas. When they stopped off at a gas station, he got out to go and pay for it.

As Bonjo and Marcela waited in the car, Bonjo glanced out of the window and saw a beautiful 600 Benz pull up to the pump across from his. The car was so nice that he didn't even focus on who the driver was. By the time he looked up, his window was being smashed and glass flew all over him.

Marcela tried to reach for the gun under her seat, but Mitch was already pointing a chrome .45 at her head.

The driver came out of the gas station and didn't know what was going on. When he got close enough to see what was happening, Mitch fired two shots, striking him in his knee and upper thigh. Mitch quickly turned the gun back on Marcela and Bonjo, who was still stunned. He pointed the gun two inches from Bonjo's face and looked into his eyes.

"Semaj is still alive, Mitch! You're killing us for nothing!" Bonjo said, copping the deuces. "She's been alive this whole fuckin' time!" he shouted.

The words cut through Mitch like a hot knife through butter. It sounded too good to be true and he was well aware of the kind of things a nigga would say right before he was about to be killed. He looked in Bonjo's eyes and saw something that made him feel that he might be telling the truth. If she was alive, he needed to know where she was immediately. "Where is she?" he asked as he pressed the gun up against Bonjo's head.

"I don't know. She's the head of the Espriella Family now," Bonjo responded.

"Yeah, she's the boss now," Marcela chimed in.

Mitch thought about it for a moment. The driver on the ground holding his leg in pain was starting to draw a crowd of people. He wasn't going to shoot Bonjo right now because he might need him in the future to help him find his daughter… if he was telling the truth. If he proved to be a liar, it wouldn't be hard to find him whenever he felt like it.

Killing was what Mitch did. He turned the gun on Marcela though, not caring much about her. He squeezed the trigger without hesitation, shooting her pointblank in the chest twice, which knocked her back up against the door. Her vest caught one of the bullets, but the other one went right through, entering with force. "That's just in case you were lying to me!" Mitch said and backed up to his car.

Mitch was pretty much heartless at this point without his baby girl, and even if the Milano Family didn't kill Semaj, he was going to make sure they paid for taking her away from him. He got into his car and pulled off.

Bonjo reached under the seat and grabbed the gun, jumped out of the car and fired at Mitch as he drove away. Several rounds busted out the back window and hit the trunk. Bonjo didn't want to lose him so he jumped in the driver's seat of the limo and sped off after him with Marcela's body in the back seat.

Three big black SUV's pulled up in front of Gio's mansion, knocking the front gate off its hinges. Flint sat in the passenger seat of the first truck, and jumped out the moment it stopped in front of the mansion. All the doors to the trucks swung open and U.S. Marshals were everywhere.

"Search warrant!" Flint yelled before knocking down the door with the battering ram.

FBI and U.S. Marshals swarmed the house with automatic rifles in hand.

Joel, one of Bonjo's men was sitting in the back yard smoking a joint when he heard all the commotion going on in the house. Once he saw FBI written on a few jackets, he took off running and leapt over the seven-foot gate like it was a two-foot hurdle. S.W.A.T. was right behind him and caught him a short distance away.

Luckily no one else was in the house, but bodies weren't what Flint was looking for. He hoped a search of the house would turn up a massive amount of evidence. Although someone tried to clean up Gio's office, there were still small traces of blood left. But Flint saw more than that. He saw blood splatter all over the legs of the desk. That prompted him to check the desk further. He found an empty safe underneath it, but that didn't stop him from searching every inch of the house.

He walked through the entire house tapping on walls looking for hollow spots, and moving every bit of furniture out of the way until most of it was sitting outside. He tore the house apart and still didn't find shit. Nobody in the family was stupid enough to hide coke in the same place they rested their head.

Flint just took a couple samples of the blood in the office, locked Joel up and left the property.

"Search warrant!" federal Agent Potter yelled as he rushed into the funeral home with a dozen other agents behind him. Several employees who were working at the time were swiftly put in handcuffs and taken outside to sit on the curb.

The federal agents searched everything on the premises. They even opened up coffins and checked inside of the dead bodies. They flipped flowerpots over, took down paintings from the walls, and bagged and tagged everything in the building that could be used for drug trafficking.

The place was rather small so the search didn't last long. The feds pretty much found nothing there either; that is until Agent Potter was about to leave the building. When he got to the exit door—the same door he rushed in—he just so happened to look to the side and saw a shadow move through a crack in the wall. He thought that he was tripping for a second until he saw it move again. He drew his weapon and yelled out for assistance from the other agents. There wasn't an apparent doorway so he didn't have any idea how to get back there. The thought of evidence being disposed of ran through his mind which made him react.

He snatched a crowbar from one of the agents and

began to tear into the crack in the wall with it. He broke a large piece of wood out of the wall and he proceeded to squeeze his body through the hole. But as soon as he did, gunfire erupted and a bullet struck him in his arm before he could pull himself out.

More shots were fired and bullets began piercing the wall, forcing the FBI agents to take cover. Some of them spilled out the front door onto the sidewalk and turned around to return fire at the wall. All the agents inside began firing round after round, knocking chunks of wood and sheetrock into the air.

Potter, who was still on the ground, wrapped his tie around his wound to stop the bleeding. He switched his gun to his other hand, sticking it inside the wall and began firing rapidly.

A bullet hit the gunman in his neck and the sound of his gun falling to the floor assured Potter that he had hit him. SWAT rushed into the hole in the wall with tactical precision and secured the area without further gunfire.

When Potter walked into the separate room adjacent to the funeral home, it was like hitting the jackpot. Several male workers were in the room cutting up large amounts of cocaine. It was everywhere, and there were more than enough to pass out life sentences to everyone in the organization. Other law enforcement officers congratulated Potter before he was taken to an ambulance to be treated for his gunshot wound.

Bonjo chased Mitch all through the city, but he couldn't get close enough to shoot at him out of the window. Mitch took him on a hell of a ride, and as Bonjo was driving, he just so happened to look in his rearview mirror and saw Marcela rolling around on the floor in the back. His decision to stop following Mitch was a hard one but he had to get Marcela to the hospital. He didn't know how badly she was hurt, but it had to be bad because she wasn't answering him when he called her name. He turned off and changed his route, and watched Mitch driving away.

He pulled up in front of the Milano's private hospital, jumped out and grabbed Marcela. There was blood all over the back seat and all over Marcela when he pulled her out of the car. She didn't have any signs of life in her, but Bonjo ran with her in his arms into the emergency room.

He was shocked when he ran straight into a group of federal agents who were standing at the door with a search warrant. His intent was to just drop her off and leave before anyone started asking questions, but that plan was cut short. The heavy blood on his shirt along with the dead-looking woman in his arms quickly got the attention of the many law enforcement officers in the building. They took Marcela's body out of his arms and immediately placed him in handcuffs without asking any questions.

Chapter 17

The bullet wound in Paris' shoulder was becoming excruciating despite the fact that the bullet went right through. She could swear that something was wrong because it was burning too much. She felt she needed to go to the hospital and before she knew it found herself pulling up right in front of one.

Before she could even park, the pain in her arm quickly went away when she saw Sosa, Semaj and Nyala coming out of the front door. She instinctively reached for the 9mm Beretta in her center console, but once she saw that there was heavy security with them, she changed her mind. Paris knew that she wouldn't last a minute in a gun battle with the many guns they were probably carrying. The women looked like they were happy, and that bothered her. She felt that Sosa should know that she was coming for her.

Paris pulled her cell phone out instead of the gun and called Ox to get some backup. She had to be careful though because she didn't want to accidentally get Nyala shot if the confrontation had to end in a gun battle. Ox wasn't answering his cell phone, and that was probably because he saw that it was her calling.

She hung right up and called Pea-Body, one of Ox's henchmen from New York. He picked up the phone right away. Pea-Body was the type that would do anything to get noticed by Ox, and if he had the opportunity to get Ox's kidnapped daughter back, he was down with whatever plan Paris came up with.

Semaj, Sosa and Nyala went to the park, a place that Nyala had never been before. Sosa just wanted to spend as much time with her as she possibly could. She might not have this opportunity again. She watched as Nyala slid down the slide. She squatted in front of it so that Nyala landed right into her arms.

The heavy security provided by Semaj was a great help as well. She had Vikingo and two other men standing close by at all times, and they all were definitely strapped to the T.

"He's watching you pretty hard," Sosa joked when she noticed the way Vikingo was hovering close to Semaj.

Semaj had to smile when she looked up and saw him standing a couple yards away. She felt well protected both physically and emotionally, and that was all that counted. He was more than just a bodyguard, but she didn't know whether or not she could call him her man at this point, although he definitely earned the title. "He's special," she said to Sosa. "So, how do you wanna deal with this situation?" she then asked, nodding at Nyala.

"I haven't thought about that too much lately. I'm just happy to have her back, Maj. One thing is for sure and two things for certain though: I'm not giving her back, so whatever happens, happens."

"You ever think about moving? I would love for you to come live wit' me," Semaj suggested.

Sosa was about to respond, but suddenly sensed tension in the air. She looked over and saw Vikingo pulling his strap from his waist and putting it down by his side. The other two guards did the same while looking off into the park at three approaching figures. Semaj saw the look in Sosa'a eyes and turned to see what was going on.

Paris, Pea-Body and another Jamaican walked up the small hill and entered the playground area. This was the first time that Semaj laid her eyes on Paris since the night at the club. She stood up, reached in the waistband at her back, pulled the Glock .40 and placed it down by her side. She started to walk towards them, but Sosa grabbed the back of her shirt and stopped her. It took everything in her not to start shooting, and if it wasn't for Nyala sitting right next to her she would have.

"I'm not coming like that," Paris said. She was about twenty yards away and had her hands in the air as she kept coming towards them. "I just want to take Nyala back home to her father. We don't have to make a scene out here."

Just her asking for Nyala had Sosa heated. Her response was to pull her gun from her waistband and place it in front of her. *Paris must be out of her fuckin' mind to think that she was going to just walk up and ask nicely for Nyala and I was going to just give her up without a fight.* "You musta bumped ya mafuckin' head! Tell Ox he can suck my dick!" Sosa yelled out.

Paris just smiled while trying to keep her cool. But she wasn't going to leave the park without the little girl. It was either that or she would die trying. Hell, she was already dead in Ox's eyes, so getting Nyala back would be her way of staying alive. She looked around to check the numbers, and saw that she was only outnumbered by two people. It was very quiet in the park. The only sounds were the birds chirping in the trees.

Paris turned as if she was going to walk away, but she spun right back around with a gun in her hand and squeezed the trigger multiple times towards them and hit one of Vikingo's men in the chest.

Sosa instinctively turned around and shielded Nyala while the Columbians opened fire on Paris and the Jakes.

Pea-Body sidestepped, pulled his gun and wildly returned fire, hitting the slide and other playground equipment.

Vikingo sidestepped with him and accurately fired two rounds into his stomach that dropped him to the ground. But that didn't stop Pea-Body from continuing to shoot, which he did and hit Vikingo in his leg.

There were bullets flying everywhere, and after seeing the up close and personal gunfight, the other Jamaican took off running in fear without firing a single shot. Paris tried to shoot him in his back for running off like a punk but she missed.

Semaj backpedaled all the way up to a tree while unleashing bullet after bullet in Paris' direction. She got to the tree and used it for cover. She dropped an empty clip and threw another in. Sosa picked up Semaj's slack. She cupped her gun in her hand and fired accurate shots Paris' way.

Paris slipped behind the jungle gym's thick wooden beam, popped the empty clip out of her gun and stuffed another one back in it. She tried to come back out firing, but Semaj had come from behind the tree, firing every last bullet she had in her gun as she walked towards her. A bullet, chipped wood off the jungle gym right in front of Paris' face. At this point she was totally outnumbered.

Pea-body had run out of bullets and Vikingo took advantage of this fact. He walked up to him and planted a bullet into the back of his head. Sosa continued firing at Paris after putting Nyala behind a tall, thick tree. By then, Vikingo and his boy were also firing down on Paris.

Four guns fired shot after shot, and the only thing that was keeping Paris alive was the twelve-inch thick wooden beam holding up the jungle gym. All she wanted to do was get the hell out of dodge at this point.

After realizing that a couple of shooters were out of bullets, she took her chances. She came from behind the beam with both hands on her gun and picked her targets before shooting. She managed to hit the other one of Vikingo's men in the head before Semaj took her down, squeezing several rounds into her legs causing her to fall to the ground. Semaj and Sosa slowly walked up to Paris with their guns still aimed at her.

Paris tried to get one last shot off, and her target was to be Semaj. When they got close enough, she quickly pointed at Semaj's face and squeezed the trigger. Semaj jumped at the sound of the gun clicking. It was empty, and for a split second she actually saw herself being shot in the face.

Sosa thought Paris was going to plead for her life, but she was wrong. Paris simply lay back on the ground with a smile on her face. She thought that if she just had one more bullet in her gun, Semaj would be lying right next to her, dead too. She didn't say a word and really didn't have a chance to as Semaj and Sosa stood above her with guns drawn.

Words couldn't explain what was going through Semaj's head at that moment. This was it; her chance at redemption. As she pointed the gun at Paris' face she could see a hint of fear in her eyes. That was all she needed to see. She pulled the trigger and sent a bullet to the center of her forehead.

Sosa then pointed her gun at Paris' head, and at the same time they both pushed seven rounds apiece into her face, neck and head, dismantling everything from the neck up. Pieces of flesh and chunks of brain matter flew everywhere, and if it wasn't for Vikingo coming over and pulling them away, they would have still been there.

Sosa grabbed Nyala and they all left the park, guns in hand.

Chapter 18

Qua had to go into the trenches in order to find Murda Mitch. Brooklyn was Mitch's stomping ground and Bed-Stuy was where he used to always hang out. He found himself hugging the stoop with the young niggas, hoping that someone had seen him. But unfortunately, Mitch remained only a legend around there.

Qua should have known that a nigga like Mitch would be hard to find, but he still went to every bar, strip club, gambling spot and fast food joint in the 'hood, hoping he would fuck around and run into him. It was a long shot, but for Qua it was well worth it.

Vikingo's face went blank after he got off the phone. Semaj thought it was from Sosa stitching up his wound, but when he gave her the saddest look in the world, she knew that it had to be something more serious. "We gotta go back to Columbia right now," he said, damn near getting up with the needle still stuck in his leg.

"What's wrong?" Semaj asked as she walked over to him as he was getting up off the kitchen table. She could see the concern in his eyes, and for a second it looked like he was about to cry. There was only thing that could make him feel that way, and a gut feeling told her that he had something to do with her grandmother. She grabbed his hand, looked into his eyes and asked him again what was wrong.

He looked like he didn't want to tell her. "It's Valentina," he said, and took the needle and thread out of Sosa's hand and began sewing his leg himself.

His words sent chills down Semaj's back. She was thinking the worst might have happened to Valentina. She had the same urge to get there as fast as she could.

"Yo, come with us," Semaj offered Sosa. She wanted to get her as far away from Ox as she could.

Sosa couldn't leave yet. She still had to take care of business before she could do anything. She knew beyond a shadow of a doubt that there was nowhere she could go that Ox wouldn't find her, and she didn't want to bring her problems to Semaj's front door. "No, I can't go wit' you, Maj. But you can take Nyala wit' you. I'll come get her when all this shit is over," she said, wanting her daughter out of harm's way.

Knowing Sosa for some time now and how she thought, Semaj understood and was happy to take Nyala to Columbia with her. Sosa was preparing for the inevitable confrontation with her baby's father, and she didn't need any distractions to prevent her from going ham.

"We pretty much know everything, man," Agent Flint said as he sat across from Bonjo in the Federal Building. "I know you've got something for us. Just give us something so you can help yourself."

"You're talking to the wrong guy. If you say you know everything, then why don't you send me over to the jail so I can be processed and on the block in time for chow?" Bongo said sarcastically.

"You know you're facing a mandatory life sentence for what we found in the funeral home and in the hospital basement. That's a guarantee. I bet my life on it that the prosecution is going to get a conviction," Flint threatened. He put every worst case scenario out there and hoped that Bonjo would crack. "All you gotta do is tell me where you get the drugs from. I'll see to it personally that you don't get any more than ten years in prison, and I'll make up the paperwork that states that you didn't cooperate," he offered.

It was a hell of an offer for someone who didn't have any loyalty to the game. Real men stand up and take their own punishment when indictments start dropping. Only weak bitch ass niggas start pointing the finger. After all, that's what every gangsta signed up for when he decided to pick the streets over the nine to five. Shit, with the information Bonjo had on Semaj and the entire 16 Tent, he could have gotten released from the building on the spot without being charged with anything! But he didn't, and that's what separated him from the boys.

"I want to call my lawyer!" Bonjo requested, ending the interrogation and sending Flint's blood pressure through the roof.

LuLu sat in the car looking up at the project building, hoping that Mitch would return. She had gotten word from a friend of the family that he was seen in these projects a couple days ago. LuLu never actually saw him coming or leaving the building, but when she noticed a Benz sitting in the project parking lot with bullet holes in the back of it, it sparked her curiosity.

She wasn't aware that Bonjo had put those holes there earlier that day, nor did she know that Mitch had killed Marcela. She just felt like it was worth waiting around to see what would happen.

At this point LuLu was on some other shit and had all kinds of crazy thoughts running through her mind. She sat in the car smoking a blunt, something she never did. She normally tried to stay on point and keep her wits sharp, but the stress of fighting her family's battles was starting to take it's toll and had her falling off.

She was just about to pull off when she noticed a familiar form coming down the B-wing steps. She still wasn't sure if it was Mitch, but she could tell his walk from anywhere, and whoever this was walked just like him. She slowly eased out of the car on the passenger side, trying to get the jump on him as soon as he emerged out the door. Once he walked under the light in the project hallway, she immediately recognized his face.

She cocked her gun back and walked across the street with it down by her side. She strolled right past a couple dudes standing in front of the building who were pitchin' work. Mitch was coming out of the building and it looked like he was heading for his car. LuLu opened fire before he got the chance to get to the parking lot.

Mitch spun around, whipping a chrome .45 from his pants pocket, looking to see where the shots was coming from. The night provided a cover for LuLu who was relentless with back-to-back shots.

By the time Mitch finally saw where the shots were coming from he had already taken one in his side. "Arrrggghhh!" he yelled and ran back into the project building. LuLu was right on his heels and ran into the building behind him and firing off another round into his back as he fled up the steps.

Mitch fell to the ground in the hallway in front of an apartment door. Turning on his back he could see LuLu coming up the stairs, and when she got in range he fired several shots at her, causing her to stumble back down the steps. Every time she tried to get to the top of the stairs, he fired another round to make sure she wasn't able to get to him. LuLu eventually had to give up. She ran back down the stairs and out of the building.

Mitch couldn't move, and if LuLu had waited twenty more seconds she would have been able to walk up on him with ease because by then he was unconscious.

Chapter 19

Semaj flew back to Columbia the same night she killed Paris, bringing Nyala along with her on the strength of Sosa. When the helicopter landed near the compound Semaj's Uncle Jorge was waiting for them in a golf cart. The ride back to the house was quiet and Jorge didn't say a word to Semaj except that Valentina wanted to talk to her.

When they pulled into the compound it seemed as if everybody from the family was there. Some were in tears and some just looked like they were in shock. Semaj thought that Valentina was dead from the way everyone was acting. Inside the house was just as packed as the outside, and people moved to the side when they saw Semaj and Vikingo heading for Valentina's bedroom where Jorge directed them to go.

Semaj directed one of her family members to take Nyala into the room where all the children were playing, in a mountain of toys. At first she was skeptical about leaving Semaj's side that was until she saw how much fun the other kids were having.

Once through the hallway Semaj walked into Valentina's bedroom. She was lying in bed, pale faced and weak. Semaj put her hands over her mouth thinking that Valentina was dead. She wasn't though. Her eyes opened when she felt Semaj's presence in the room. Semaj gently climbed onto the bed and sat next to her.

"I knew you were coming," Valentina said weakly as she looked up at Semaj.

"What's going on?" Semaj asked, confused as hell. She hadn't been gone but for a couple days, and when she left Valentina looked healthy as ever. She had no signs of sickness and she definitely didn't tell her that something was wrong with her.

"Six months ago I was diagnosed with a rare heart disease that is incurable. The doctors told me that I only had six months to live," she struggled to get out. "I guess he was mistaken," she chuckled.

The tears started pouring out of Semaj's eyes. This was a tough blow considering the fact that she just found out that Valentina was her grandmother. She started thinking about all the things she didn't get a chance to do with her and all the things she won't be able to learn from her. It was like an emotional rush and it was devastating.

"Now, don't you go crying on me," she said, painfully reaching up and placing her hand on Semaj's face.

Semaj grabbed her hand, kissed it and held it up against her face. She didn't know if this would be the last time she would ever feel her touch again so she wanted to cherish every moment they had. Looking at Valentina reminded Semaj so much of her mother. Everything from her looks to the way she talked was a heart wrenching reminder of where she came from.

"I want you to know that you will be the boss of this family when I go."

"You're not gonna die, Grandma!"

"Sshh! Yes, I am gonna die, and when I do you're going to be head of this family. Be smart and listen to your Uncle Jorge. He loves you just like I love you."

"Grandma, please don't go!" Semaj cried out.

"My life is complete. I have accomplished the one goal in the world I wanted to before I passed..." Valentina said, going in and out of consciousness.

"What's that, Grandma? What's that?" Semaj asked, trying to keep her awake and with her.

It was silent in the room for a while, and even Vikingo was shedding tears at this point. Everybody thought that she was gone but then Semaj leaned in closer to kiss her.

"I found you." Valentina said with her last breath before her body shut down completely.

Semaj began sobbing, and so did everybody else in the room. The Queen had passed away and this was catastrophic for the Espriella Family. Semaj gave her grandmother one final kiss before getting up and leaving the room. That was all she had the strength to do.

If it wasn't for the numerous police sitting outside in front of the project building, LuLu would have run over to the EMT's while they were bringing Mitch out and put several more bullets in his head. It took her a minute to debate whether or not she should do it. She couldn't believe that he was still alive as she watched from across the street as they loaded him into the back of the ambulance. She was sure she hit him in his chest and in his back.

She got on the phone and called Emilia to establish the fact that she wasn't going back to Santo Domingo. Emilia was pretty much trying to force her and Sosa back home in order to preserve the rest of their lives. From the way things were going they were sure to end up dead just like everybody else in the family.

But LuLu had other plans. She wasn't going back. She was starting to feel like it was her time to take over the family, and she swore to herself that she could do a better job than Gio, Paulie or Ortiz ever did. She had killed many people and sold much cocaine. She didn't come this far just to turn on her heels and run back home. That wasn't in the plan.

Qua tossed the cigarette to the side and walked into the barbershop, a place he hadn't been to in years. The old barbers weren't there anymore but the owner was the same. He was his longtime friend since elementary school, Tito. What's good wit' you, playboy?" Qua said, walking up to Tito who had a head in his chair. "After all these years you telling me you still cuttin' hair?" he joked.

Tito was happy to see his man. It had been a while since Qua been in the 'hood. He was 'hood official, but money and drama was what got him to migrate to London. Just seeing him back was cool with Tito, but he wondered what the visit was for, considering Qua just popped up out of nowhere. He knew Qua well enough to know when he was up to something, even after not seeing him for a while.

"Aye, I need to holla at you about something," Qua said, pulling Tito to the side after he finished with his customer.

"Some shit never changes!" Tito said with a smirk.

"Aye, you seen Murda Mitch?" he asked with a funny look on his face and not holding eye contact.

"All got-damn day!" Tito shot back with a chuckle. That was an easy question to answer considering he'd been on the news all night as the shooting victim over at the projects. Tito didn't have to say a word. He was sure that if he turned on the TV it would still be on the news. He did, and it took a few minutes but to no surprise, the news camera was showing Mitch's face on the screen.

Qua was stunned by the large photo of Mitch's face covering the TV screen. What was more disturbing was that somebody had gotten to him before Qua could, but from the looks of things, whoever it was didn't finish the job.

By the time Tito had turned around from putting the remote control on the counter Qua was out the door. If given the opportunity, he was going to make sure the job got finished.

Semaj got a phone call around one in the morning, waking her up from her sleep. It was Sosa calling. She sat up in her bed and looked over at Vikingo who was still asleep. She hadn't left the compound since they took Valentina's body to the church to be cleansed before the funeral. She answered the phone in a low voice. By the way Sosa breathed heavily into the phone before saying anything, she could tell that something was wrong.

"Ya pops is in the hospital," Sosa told her while standing in the waiting area of the hospital. "This shit's been on the news all day. He got shot like twice in the projects a few hours ago."

"What?" Semaj was shocked. "Are you serious?" she asked with an attitude.

"Yeah. I don't know who did it but I'ma stay at the hospital until you get here."

"Thanks, Cousin. I'll be there in a couple of hours," Semaj informed her and hung up the phone.

The jet was gassed up but the pilot wouldn't be

available until around six, a mere five hours from now. Valentina's funeral was in a couple of days so that gave her enough time to get back to the States, check on her father and make it back in time for the service. *Damn! I hope he's okay!* she thought to herself as she climbed back into bed next to Vikingo.

Mitch's shooting wasn't the only thing blazing through the news all night. Sosa watched as federal agents swarmed the hospital, the funeral home and Gio's place in one of New York's biggest raids. They had pictures of several key people in the Milano Family that were a part of the conspiracy to distribute large amounts of cocaine throughout the New York/New Jersey area. The news anchor called the Milano Family a 'Mafia'. They named a lot of people, like Gio, Paulie, Ortiz and Bonjo as being the heads of the family. They even showed pictures of Bonjo coming out of the family's hospital in handcuffs and a shirt stained with blood.

Sosa had no idea that any of this was going on, and because of them not getting into specifics she didn't know that her sister, Marcela was dead. She just sat in the waiting room glued to the TV to make sure that her name didn't pop up, because if it did she was out.

Her cell phone ringing brought her out of her daze. She looked down at her phone and it was Emilia. "Yo!"

she answered without taking her eyes off the TV.

"Are you watching the news?" Emilia asked. She was sitting in her hotel room watching the news herself.

"Yeah. This shit is crazy! You think they got Marcela too?" Sosa asked.

"Nah. We won't know anything until Bonjo calls… that's if he calls. I'm telling you, Sis, we got to get the hell out of here," Emilia said with all seriousness.

"Yeah, I hear you. Have you spoken to LuLu?"

"She just called me crying. She told me to come pick her up from somewhere in Brooklyn. I'm about to go get her and I'll call you back when she's with me."

"Alright, do that. I gotta go right now," Sosa said, seeing doctors rushing back into the emergency room where Mitch was. "Make sure you call me the moment you got her," she stressed, before hanging up.

Chapter 20

Emilia pulled up to the crab shack to pick up LuLu. She was standing out front and quickly jumped into the car once she saw Emilia. Emilia glanced at LuLu and something seemed off about her. She appeared to be high and couldn't keep her nose from running. She also had dark circles under her eyes like she hadn't slept in days. This was another reason why Emilia felt it was time to get out of the States and head back to Santo Domingo. The City of New York had literally torn the family apart, and she felt that if they stayed any longer there wouldn't be a Milano Family left.

"I set up the flight for us to go back to Santo Domingo. We're leaving tomorrow," Emilia said, looking off into the road ahead of her. "There's nothing left here for us, LuLu. Do you hear what I'm saying?" she snapped because LuLu wasn't paying any attention to her.

But LuLu heard every word she said and had no desire to go back to Santo Domingo. She had weighed the pros and the cons and staying in New York was the conclusion LuLu came to. She felt like at this point she didn't have to listen to anybody, and if necessary she could carry the Milano name on by herself. "I'm not going back, Em. I'm stayin' here," she responded with an attitude. "There ain't shit in Santo Domingo for me. And what da fuck are we running from?"

"What are you talking about, LuLu? Everybody is dead! Gio, Paulie, Ortiz, JahJah and Marcela!"

"Marcela?" LuLu asked, stunned to hear the news about Marcela's death.

"Yeah, Marcela's dead too, and so will you be if you stay here. You got the Jamaicans running around out here, and you still got Mitch…"

"Fuck Mitch!" LuLu shot back. She was still angry that he wasn't dead after she shot him. "I don't give a fuck about none of them!"

It got quiet in the car for a moment. Everything from last night started running through LuLu's head and she was getting tired of hearing the complaints from Emilia and the weakness in her voice. It only proved that she shouldn't even be considered to be the one to lead the family.

"Look, Lu. I'm the boss of this family now. Everybody is dead and Bonjo is in federal custody. I'm telling you that you're going back with me tomorrow, and there's no negotiating this," Emilia spit with a serious look on her face.

"The boss? Oh, you're the boss now?" LuLu said sarcastically. She sat there and thought about it, and Emilia was the next in line to be the boss.

Thinking ahead a little further, LuLu realized that

she would have been the last person in the family to be the boss, considering she was the youngest out of the Milano sisters. It would have been Marcela, Emilia, Sosa and then her. Bonjo was locked up so he couldn't claim the reins. This meant that the family name rested on the last Milano standing, and LuLu wasn't about to let her chances of being the boss of the family go. Without thinking any further, she reached for Emilia's gun that was sitting on the center console.

Emilia turned toward her sister and couldn't believe she had the gun pointed directly at her head. She was so pissed Emilia swerved off the road trying to pull over. "Lu, have you lost ya fuckin' mind or something?" Emilia barked, throwing the car in park. "Fuck is you gonna do wit' that, Lu? Shoot me?" She laughed, not taking her seriously.

LuLu just stared at her with hate filled eyes. She realized that there was no turning back at this point. It wasn't until LuLu didn't break the stare that Emilia knew that she was about to be murdered by her own sister.

"It's my turn now, Sis," LuLu said and took the safety off the gun. Emilia tried to reach for the weapon but LuLu was too fast. She closed one eye before squeezing the trigger. The bullet went through Emilia's face, busting her head wide open. The shot was so loud inside of the car that it burst a blood vessel in LuLu's right ear, sending a sharp pain through her body. She sat there and looked at Emilia and the blood coming from her head and couldn't believe she actually went through with it.

With little traffic passing by she got out of the car and left Emilia on the side of the road.

Semaj looked out of the small window in the jet, and the sight of the rising sun mixed with being wrapped in Vikingo's arms made the morning complete. She was anxious to see her father again but she wished it were under better circumstances.

Thinking about her father made Semaj take perspective on everything that had transpired over the past few months. She was on her way to being one of the biggest drug distributers in the world. The entire East Coat was hers, half of the West Coast, and recently a few States down south had become high-end clients. London was only a brick away from being hers, and growing cocaine fields in South America was only a couple business meetings away.

"I need to talk to you," Vikingo said, placing his chin on Semaj's shoulder.

"Yeah, what's up, *papi?*" she asked in her best Spanish accent.

Vikingo smiled not because *"papi"* was the only word Semaj knew in Spanish but because she sounded so good saying it. "I know that this might sound crazy and I hope you don't look at me like I'm a psycho, but… *yo necisito tu para mi esposa,*" he said in Spanish.

She didn't know what the hell he just said and playfully pinched his arm for him to say it in English.

He laughed for a second before becoming serious again. "I need you to be my wife," he spoke ever so softly into her ear.

Semaj turned to look at him to make sure he was serious. The thought of marriage only crossed her mind one time in her life and that was when she was with Qua. She didn't know what to say or even if she felt the same way. He hit her with this out of nowhere and for a second she was stunned. "Did you just say that you wanna marry me?" she asked. She heard him correctly the first time but wanted to hear it from him again, preferably in Spanish.

"No, *mami*. I didn't say I wanted to marry you, I said that I *need* to marry you. There's a difference between *want* and *need*. When you want something that just means it's something that you desire to have. But when you need something that means you can't do without it," he said, making it clear. "So when I say that I need you to be my wife that means that I can't be without you," he professed, looking into her eyes.

Semaj's heart melted and everything inside of her told her to believe him. She couldn't find any reason why she shouldn't marry Vikingo except that she was still in love with Qua. Semaj never thought it was possible to be in love with two men at the same time until now. But Qua seemed so out of reach for her and she wasn't confident that after all they had been through that they could find their way back to each other. On the other hand Vikingo was the type of man that she could see herself spending the rest of her life with. When they were together he always made Semaj feel like she was all that mattered to him. He was handsome, he was a protector and he damn sure knew how to make love to her. What else could she ask for? She only lived once and she was willing to jump. "I'll be your wife, Vikingo! But if you hurt me… I swear that if you hurt me, I will kill you myself and bury your body in a coca field!" she joked with tears in her eyes. "And where the hell is my ring? How are you gonna ask me to marry you and you ain't got no ring?" she snapped, wiggling her finger in his face.

He couldn't help laughing at her, but to him a ring was the smallest token of showing a woman that you want to spend the rest of your life with her. What he had was bigger than any ring a man could ever put on a woman's finger. What he had was true love within his heart, and it was the kind of love that could only be found in the soul.

Sosa sat in Mitch's hospital room and watched him slowly dying. She had to be honest with herself looking down at the man who killed her uncle and her good friend, JahJah. She wanted to kill him, but the only thing that was stopping her was that he was Semaj's father, and the fact that there were cops hovering outside the room. The love she had for Semaj was crazy, and at times it was stronger than the love she had for her own flesh and blood sisters. She wasn't going to be the one to hurt her like that.

Mitch wasn't the only person that was on her mind either. She was trying to figure out why Ox hadn't struck yet. It wasn't like him, and Sosa expected for the whole world to come crashing down when he came to get his daughter, especially if he loved her as much as she did. In a way she was expecting to be killed by Ox, but at the same time if she was going to die, there were going to be a lot of mufuckas dying with her.

When Qua walked into the hospital he damn near turned around when he saw all the cops standing around. He didn't even make it to the emergency room, let alone to Mitch's room. It was like a mini police station in there and Qua knew that he wasn't going to be able to do anything right now. It burned him up though to have to walk out that hospital without Mitch being a dead man. As soon as the heat cooled down a bit, he would be back. Right now his best bet was to get the hell out of the hospital because one pat-down search would put him in jail.

Chapter 21

Semaj walked into the hospital closely eyeing her surroundings. There were cops everywhere, especially around a certain room. She walked towards that room and an officer stopped her right in front of Mitch's door. She immediately identified herself as his daughter and was admitted inside. She warned the officers to be on the lookout for any dread headed Jamaicans because they might have been the ones who shot him.

Once she got into the room she almost fainted when she saw her father lying on the bed with all kinds of tubes and cables sticking out of him. He wasn't able to breathe on his own so he was hooked up to a respirator. He looked bad but she was happy to see him still alive. Semaj couldn't stop crying noticing all scars on his body

It wasn't long before the doctor came into the room with an x-ray of his upper body. He explained to Semaj how serious his injuries were and that there was a possibility he wouldn't make it through the night. The option for her to be the one to pull the plug was given to her, which she declined.

Semaj wouldn't have been strong enough to do it.

"He's not going to die. Mitch is a warrior," Sosa told her and wiped the tears from Semaj's face. "You gotta be strong and ask God to give him another chance."

Semaj just sat there staring at the heart monitor. Sosa sat there too but she happened to look up at the TV in Mitch's room, and caught a story that was breaking on the news:

> "...A woman was found this morning dumped on the side of the road with what appears to be a gunshot to her head. Our live reporter, Max is on the scene with the latest."
>
> "Yes, Karen, I'm standing here on this quiet street where the victim whose name is being withheld was shot in the head sometime late last night..."

The cameraman focused on a car in the background, and Sosa almost vomited at the sight of Emilia's red Dodge Charger with yellow crime scene tape around it. She knew it was Emilia's because of the Tasmanian devil doll in the back window.

Semaj's heart dropped at seeing the dismay on Sosa's face. She looked up at the TV and also noticed that it was Emilia's car. Sosa decided to answer her phone that had been ringing off and on for the past couple hours, hoping to get some information about the shooting.

"What's up, Sosa? Was that Em?" Semaj asked, hoping that there was some other woman's dead body in the car.

"That was LuLu. She wants me to come pick her up. I

swear, something just ain't right!"

"You need me to come wit' you?" Semaj asked, seeing the concern in Sosa's eyes.

"You gotta stay here wit' ya pops. I should be alright," Sosa said, waving her off.

"Vikingo can stay here with him and I can go with you. I don't want you rolling around out there by yourself," she said, thinking about Ox.

Vikingo wasn't too fond of the idea and put up a protest. It was no use because before he could say another word, Semaj was heading out of the room with Sosa.

Sitting at a red light two blocks away from the old morgue, Sosa took one of the two Glock .40's out of her pocketbook and checked to make sure there was a bullet in the chamber before setting it on her lap. Semaj watched her and it prompted her to reach for her gun and do the same.

They pulled up to the morgue and Sosa told Semaj to blow the horn, which she did. LuLu didn't come out and Sosa wondered why she would tell her to pick her up from here out of all places. Suspicion was running high. Sosa got out of the car with her gun in hand. This was the first time she'd seen the morgue since Bonjo told her that it had gotten burned down. The damage was still obvious and the smell of burnt wood was still heavy in the air.

Semaj also got out of the car, gun in hand, and took a

good look around the outer perimeter. "I'ma go around the back to see if I see her," she said.

Sosa nodded then preceded to the front door. When she walked in she could smell the strong aroma of weed floating through the air. She knew it had to be Ox, so she raised her gun and aimed it as she walked through the building.

She got to a section in the middle of the morgue and walked up to LuLu, who was sitting on a desk with a pistol next to her, smoking a Dutch full of haze. She had a crazy look on her face the moment Sosa entered the room. Sosa looked around to make sure LuLu was by herself before tucking her gun back in her waistband. "Lu, what's goin' on? And why are you in here?" she asked as she walked up to her.

LuLu's reaction took Sosa by surprise. She grabbed the gun off the desk and pointed it at her. Sosa jumped, not knowing if she was going to shoot her. Observing her a little closer, Sosa could see a bandage on her right ear. She could also tell by the empty Christian Brothers bottle on the floor in front of her that she had to be drunk or either crazy to point a gun in her direction.

LuLu cocked her head to the side and said in a creepy voice, "Hi, Sister-r-r-r!"

"Yo, what da fuck is wrong wit' you?" Sosa asked as she walked a little closer. LuLu jerked the gun at her to let her know not to take another step.

LuLu wasn't LuLu anymore, and Sosa was starting to see that. "What happened to Em, LuLu?" She began to think that she had something to do with her murder.

"She tried to take me back to Santo Domingo. I told her I wasn't going because New York was where I belonged. She made me do it!" LuLu said, and took another puff before tossing the Dutch to the ground.

"What did you do?" Sosa asked calmly, now trying to back up out of the room.

LuLu jumped up, keeping her gun aimed at her. She didn't have plans on letting Sosa walk out of the building alive. Her mind was made up to kill her the moment she had killed Emilia. She was too far gone now. "You know she said that she was the boss now that everybody else was dead and Bonjo was in jail. Who made her the boss?" LuLu yelled. "I can be the boss. Don't you think I can be the boss?"

"You call this being a boss? You call what you're doing being a leader? So now what, you gonna kill me too? Is that ya plan?"

"There can only be one boss."

LuLu was about to pull the trigger until she felt a gun pressed up against her head. She was shocked because she thought that they were all alone. Her injured ear made it hard for her to hear Semaj creep up from behind. Nevertheless, she kept her gun pointed at Sosa, not budging a bit by the sudden change of events. If she was going to die, she was going to take her sister with her. "Yeaaah, you still riding wit' this bitch, huh?" LuLu asked as she watched Semaj walk into her view.

"LuLu, put da, fuckin' gun down!" Semaj threatened while holding a firm grip on the .45 ACP.

"See, she's da fuckin problem now," LuLu said referring to Semaj. "She's the reason why shit is like it is. Ever since y'all let this bitch into the family people have been turning up dead. She's like a fuckin' cancer and you want her to be ya fuckin' boss? Oh, I forgot. She's y'alls' little princess!" she snapped. "Oh, and how's ya dad?" she asked Semaj with a sinister grin on her face.

Semaj looked confused. Then it hit her like a ton of bricks. *It was her! This loco bitch is responsible for my father being in the hospital fighting for his life!* She gripped the gun tighter and aimed it closer to LuLu's head.

Sosa saw that things were escalating. "LuLu, don't do this!" she pleaded.

"Fuck this bitch! Let her pull da trigger! You're da boss so make a boss call! You kill me, I kill her!" she threatened Semaj.

"Don't do this shit, LuLu!" Sosa pleaded again.

The entire room got quiet. It was so quiet that Semaj could hear her heart beating in her chest. She looked at Sosa, LuLu looked at Sosa, and Sosa looked at Semaj. A tear dropped from Semaj's eye. She knew that LuLu was about to force her hand.

Sosa looked at Semaj and just put her head down because she knew what LuLu was about to do. She closed her eyes and braced herself for impact.

But LuLu's hatred for Semaj consumed her and made her change things up. Nothing else mattered to LuLu at that moment except blowing Semaj's brains out. She spun around as fast as she could and turned her gun on Semaj but Semaj was already one step ahead of her enemy.

She didn't hesitate to pull the trigger before LuLu could get a shot off. The hollow point bullet entered her right temple and exited out the other side of her head. LuLu was dead on impact, and as her lifeless body went limp, Sosa opened her eyes just in time to see her hit the ground. She looked over at Semaj, who was standing there with sorrow in her eyes. The last person in the world she wanted to kill was LuLu, because no matter how you look at it or perceive the situation, she was family.

Semaj and Sosa finally got back to the hospital, and as soon as they walked through the doors they could hear commotion coming from the emergency room. The sight of nurses and doctors running towards her father's room caught her attention. She and Sosa took off running right behind them.

Vikingo stopped her at the door. He'd been kicked out of Mitch's room so the doctors could have room to work on him. Semaj fought her way out of his arms and ended up falling into the room. The heart monitor had flat lined and the doctor was rubbing the paddles together in order to try and shock Mitch's heart.

"Clear!" the doctor yelled, and sent two hundred volts

of electricity into Mitch's body.

"Dad-y-y-y-y!" Semaj cried out as she stood off to the side. "Please don't die, Daddy! Fight! Fight!" she screamed at the top of her lungs. "Daddy, please don't leave me!" she yelled out again.

"Clear!" the doctor yelled again, and zapped more electricity into Murda Mitch.

Vikingo wrapped Semaj in his arms and placed her head on his chest. The more she looked at the doctors working on him the more painful it was for her. The doctor stopped shocking him then looked at his watch.

Sosa eventually came into the room and rubbed Semaj's back. She couldn't help but to cry with her because she knew the feeling of losing a father.

"Don't stop! Don't stop!" Semaj cried out, jumping up and down in Vikingo's arms.

"Time of death..." the doctor began to pronounce.

"Beep... beeb... beep...!"

The heart monitor started back up again. The doctor looked astonished before he got right back to work on him, trying to maintain Mitch's heartbeat.

Semaj looked on but her body couldn't take any more. She had been through so much in the last few days that she neglected the things her body needed. That combined with the stress, she passed out right in Vikingo's arms. Her body just went limp, and before they knew it, Vikingo and Sosa were calling for medical attention for her.

Chapter 22

Semaj woke up in a hospital room groggy and thirsty, and the first person she saw was Vikingo sitting next to her bed. He hadn't moved since the doctor stabilized her. She had a stress induced panic attack that caused her body to shut down. Semaj sat up in the bed and the first thing she said to Vikingo was, "My dad?"

"He's still in the ICU. He's got the doctor scratching his head right now. They thought he was dead. Boy, I would have hated to be on his bad side if he was alive and well!" Vikingo joked, thinking about how much Mitch was fighting to stay alive.

Mitch was like the last of a dying breed. They didn't make them like him anymore. He was the definition of the word "warrior" in every sense, and when it came down to it, it was going to take a lot more than two bullets to the back and his side for his clock to stop ticking for good.

Semaj got to her feet and was escorted to the ICU area where Mitch was. The heart monitor was beeping steadily but his condition still seemed grim. Semaj pulled up a chair and sat next to him, bowed her head and closed her eyes in prayer. She begged God to spare his life and to forgive him for his sins.

Unexpectedly, Qua walked in and stood by the door. Semaj was surprised to see him standing there and wondered what he wanted. In her eyes it could only be one of two things; he was coming to see the man that killed his father die, or he was there to finish the job. Either way, he had her undivided attention. "What are you here for, Quasim?" she asked, getting up from her chair and backing up into Vikingo's arms. She only did that to be able to grab the gun in Vikingo's waistband if she had to in order to shoot Qua if he came for anything other than peace. By the look he had in his eyes, she knew that he wasn't there for peace. She knew him and his body language all too well.

Qua watched as Semaj backed into Vikingo's arms as though he was her protector. The way that he held her was that of a man who was protecting his woman. He had to admit that he was jealous, and all the old feelings he had for her were coming to the surface. He was there to make sure that Mitch didn't survive the shooting, but seeing Semaj there changed everything at that moment. "Oh, so we're using our whole names now?" he smiled. "I just came by to see how you were doing," he lied, inching his way into the room.

Semaj reached for Vikingo's gun, not really feeling Qua's vibe at all. She wasn't about to take any more chances with anybody who she felt was a threat to her or to her father.

Qua wasn't stupid though. He could see what Semaj was doing, and although he had a gun and a silencer on him he wasn't about to start a shootout in the middle of the hospital with cops walking around everywhere. He was bound to go to jail for that. But at the same time Quasim was torn. Part of him wasn't willing to let Mitch leave the hospital alive under any circumstances, but the other part that was still in love with Semaj made him want to turn around and walk out the door.

"Hold up, cowgirl! I just want to talk," he said, playfully placing his hands in the air. "Honestly, I just wanna holla at you."

Cautious but intrigued to hear what Qua wanted to talk about, Semaj let go of Vikingo's gun and slowly walked across the room to him. He opened his arms for a hug, but Semaj stuck her hand out and pushed him out into the hallway. Vikingo watched intensely as the two walked out the room.

"What you want Qua?" she asked, trying not to look him in his eyes. Semaj knew how deep her feelings ran for Qua and she had to be strong. As much as she loved him she loved her father more and if a decision had to be made who would live or die she was riding with her daddy.

Qua noticed that Semaj was going out her way to avoid making eye contact by either looking down at the floor or at the nurses and doctors passing by. "So who's that, ya boyfriend?" he asked, looking over at Vikingo standing there with the rock face on.

"Don't start ya shit right now, Qua."

"Don't start? Damn! You givin' my love away?" he asked, trying to get her to look at him.

She almost didn't want to answer the question, but decided if she told Qua the truth maybe it would somehow break the hold he still had on her heart. "He's my fiancé," she answered.

Qua felt like he had just been sucker punched in the gut. The sudden pain in the pit of his stomach fucked his head up. It was the kind of hurt that he didn't expect, considering he was there to kill her father. If he had it his way, he would have killed Mitch without anybody knowing it was him, and still tried to rebuild his relationship with Semaj. "So, you telling me that it's that easy for you to forget about what we had? Are you saying that you don't love me no more, Maj?"

"You've got a girlfriend, Qua. Yeah, I saw you kissing her at the Tent meeting," she shot back.

"What was I suppose to do? You left Jamaica and I haven't heard from you since. I waited and waited for you to call me and you never did. Fuck! I even thought that you might come through London to visit, but you never came. What was I supposed to do?" he yelled out letting his anger get the best of him.

It was obvious that there were a lot of unsolved issues between the two of them and Semaj was beginning to feel guilty because he was right. She was the one who cut herself off from the outside world when she was on

Valentina's compound. She was the one in the relationship who was doing all the hurting. She was the one who opened herself up to Vikingo without knowing if she and Qua were ever going to make it work. Semaj was starting to realize how she had jumped the gun getting involved with Vikingo, but he came into her life when she felt vulnerable and needed love. Valentina warned her to make sure the first door was closed before opening up another but Semaj didn't listen.

She let herself look into Qua's eyes and it was like their entire history flashed before her; their first date, the first time they made love and the overwhelming pain she was in when she thought he was dead. Qua was her first true love and regardless of what happened between them a part of her heart would always belong to him.

And for Qua the feeling was mutual. After everything she put him through he wanted her back… so much so that he was almost willing to let Mitch live in order to be with her.

The love they shared ran deep but Semaj couldn't shake her apprehension. Deep down inside a voice kept screaming at her that it could never work. Too much had transpired between them, and she would be a fool to think that Qua would ever get over Mitch killing his father. It was one thing for Qua to forgive her and let it go when they believed Murda Mitch was dead but now that he was alive, that changed the game. "Qua, it's over between me and you. We have to let it go," Semaj finally said. It almost killed her to let those words leave her mouth but in her heart she felt she was saving both of them from a lot of pain and heartache.

Qua was crushed to hear Semaj say it was over. He believed their love could get them through the bullshit but now he had to accept he was wrong.

"Have it your way," he stated in a cold, unemotional tone, trying to cover up the pain he was in. Qua took a couple steps back and walked off without saying another word.

Qua walked right past Sosa who was sitting on a chair in the hallway. When she saw him leaving she got up and went to find out what was said. "Is everything cool, Maj?"

"Yeah, everything's cool. I had to make a decision that was best for the family and it was a lot harder than I thought it would be. But I know I did the right thing and that's what matters," she told Sosa before going back into the room with her father. Although he didn't say it, Semaj could see the hurt in Qua's eyes before he left. Plus, if he was even in half the agony that Semaj was in, she knew it was bad because it damn sure was for her.

On his way out of the ICU, Qua decided that for now he would let Semaj go but he promised himself that no matter what he had to do he would win her back. He believed their love was worth it.

"So what are you going to do?" Vikingo asked Semaj as she rested her head on his shoulder.

"As soon as he gets stable enough I'm going to bring him home with us."

Many things ran through her mind during the time she sat in the hospital. Now that she was the head of an international drug conglomerate she had bigger and more serious responsibilities in her life. She could no longer continue to put herself in harm's way being careless and reckless by exposing herself to her enemies. She not only had to worry about the enemies that already existed, she had to watch out for those that were developing.

Semaj looked at her father lying in the bed. She wanted to salvage what family she did have left, and if that meant relocating them somewhere outside of the United States, then that's what she planned to do. Money definitely wasn't an issue because she inherited enough to buy her own island if she wanted to. That's why if and when Mitch was stable she was going to fly him out of here. An extraction plan was already in place, waiting for the okay to come get her father.

Sosa was also coming. The one thing Sosa would never have to worry about was money, because Semaj was going to make sure that she and Nyala were well taken care of. She wasn't going to leave her stranded, and had already made up her mind and put a million-dollar cash bounty on Ox's head so that once he was dead she wouldn't have to worry about him ever coming after her and Nyala again.

Chapter 23

It seemed like silence was always the beginning of a war, and the only sound in the room on the ICU floor was that of patients' heart monitors. Semaj had slipped off into a five-minute catnap with her head resting on her father's bed. A sudden commotion in the hallway was what woke her up, and when she got up and looked out the door to check on Sosa, she could see medical staff running down the hall. At first she thought that it was another patient's heart monitor flat lining, but the sound of a man yelling out, "Oh shit! Oh shit! He was like that when I came in here!" Semaj knew that it was something else.

Sosa, who was also taking a nap on the bench in the hallway, was woken up by all the commotion. She looked down the hallway and yawned, then looked up at the clock to see what time it was.

"What's going on?" Semaj asked her when she came out into the hallway.

"I don't know, but I saw the cops running down

there," Sosa said and stood up to stretch.

On the same floor but in another wing of the hospital, Ox turned the corner and walked down the hallway. He already left one casualty dead in the ICU on his mission to murder Sosa and anybody else that got in his way. As he passed the elevator, the door opened and out came two shorthaired Jamaicans. At the same time the elevator doors opened up on the other side of the hallway where the police were, and out walked two other Jamaicans with short haircuts. Because the cops were looking out for dread headed Jamaicans, cutting off their dreads was the only way they could get into the hospital without drawing attention to themselves. They walked right past the cops and medical staff who were tending to the dead body.

When Sosa saw the two men coming down the hall she didn't pay them any mind until she noticed the stone cold look on their faces. She looked back down the other end of the hall and could see three more men approaching. Her heart damn near busted out of her chest when she saw the gun being drawn from one of the men's suit jacket pocket.

Looking a little closer, she almost couldn't believe her eyes. She was staring at a dread-less Ox walking towards her with a gun in his hand. For a second she believed her heart stopped. Semaj didn't notice what was going on until the other Jamaicans coming down the hall pulled out guns from underneath their shirts.

"Everybody, get down!" Sosa yelled out as she saw the hit unfolding. She leaped from the bench, pulled one of the twin Glock .40's from her pocketbook and dove behind the nurse's station directly across from Mitch's room. It was in the nick of time because multiple gunshots began sounding off throughout the ICU.

A couple nurses that were at their desk dropped to the ground once the shots went off. The cops who were attending to the dead body had drawn their weapons and proceeded down the hall towards the ICU.

The bullets that were fired in Semaj's direction forced her to fall backwards to the floor. She just avoided a head shot by three inches.

Vikingo got out of his chair, crawled over to Semaj and pulled her further into the room. He pushed Mitch's bed to the other side of the room so that he was away from the door and the windows.

"Maj!" Sosa yelled out while pulling the other twin Glock from her pocketbook and sliding it across the hallway and into the room.

At this point the Jamaicans had spread out across the ICU, firing rapidly into the nurse's station. The first Jamaican jumped onto the counter and ran down it as he fired wildly at Sosa who was lying on the floor. She calmly aimed and tapped the trigger twice, hitting him in his chest and neck and knocking him off the counter. He fell to the floor face-first, shaking and going into convulsions.

In a split second, the ICU got quiet. It was like everybody was trying to preserve their ammo or at least wait to get off a good shot.

Ox crept around the back end of the nurse's station where he had Mitch's room in sight. He fired several rounds into the room, breaking the glass window next to the door.

Vikingo darted out of the room shooting at Ox as he sidestepped into the room next door. He wanted to draw some of the attention away from Mitch's room. Semaj stood in front of Mitch's bed, also returning fire every time a Jamaican popped his head up.

Officer Shark and his partner crept up to the ICU area with their guns pointed in front of them. "Put the gun down!" the officer yelled when he saw one of Ox's boys kneeling down behind the soda machine.

The second Jamaican turned around and started shooting at the cops, at which time both officers returned fire and took him down. While they shot at him, another Jamaican shot at the officers and hit Shark's partner in his groin. He instantly dropped to the floor but kept his weapon in his hand.

In a flash, the ICU became a war zone. The third Jamaican was shooting it out with Vikingo; the forth was shooting it out with the cops; the fifth was shooting it out with Semaj; and Ox was steadily creeping over to where Sosa was. At that point he didn't even want his daughter back. All he wanted to do was kill Sosa.

Again the ICU became silent and gun smoke filled the air. Everybody took this opportunity to reload. You could hear the sounds of clips falling to the floor and guns being cocked.

Sosa slid Semaj her extra clip, having only fired a couple of rounds out of her gun thus far. Before you knew it, the gun battle was back on, starting with the third Jamaican popping up from behind the counter and shooting at Vikingo.

Shark's partner seized the opportunity and released several bullets into the third Jamaican's direction. A bullet hit him in his waist and the side of his knee.

"Aah-h-h-h-h!" the forth Jamaican yelled as he sprang from behind the vending machine, gunning for the cop that just shot his boy. He was silenced by Semaj opening the side of his head with a hollow point bullet.

Shark's partner looked over at Mitch's room and wondered who had possibly saved his life, as he couldn't see Semaj. Sosa got on the move, crawling on her stomach around to the other side of the counter. She had no idea how close Ox was to walking right over to her. Only a partition separated the two, and as Ox got closer to coming around the partition, he got down on his knees and also crawled.

The forth Jamaican stood up from behind the counter and fired at Vikingo as he backed up to the emergency exit door in the far corner.

Shark pulled his partner further down the hallway and out of the line of fire and then proceeded back to the ICU area where he walked past Mitch's room. The fifth Jamaican bolted down the hallway shooting at Shark, who backed right up into Mitch's room. He felt the back of his head press up against Semaj's gun, and right then he knew that he was dead.

"I'm only tryin' to protect my father!" Semaj said. She lowered her weapon and pushed him back out into the empty hallway.

Shark saw the fifth Jamaican running down the hallway so he took off right behind him hoping to catch him before he got to the elevator. The forth Jamaican went out of the emergency exit into the stairwell, firing a few shots before the door closed behind him.

Sosa was just about to get up when she heard the gunfire subside, but instead she just so happened to look down at the ground. The partition was elevated off the ground about an inch or two, so she was able to see a shadow moving on the other side of it.

Ox slowly crept around to the end of the partition, and when he stuck his head around it to see if Sosa was on the other side he ran right into her. She was looking down the barrel of his gun. He placed the barrel up against the partition and aimed it at her head. "Die, bitch!" He exhaled and closed his eyes.

"Fuck you, Ox!" she said and pulled the trigger, planting a bullet in the center of his head.

Ox squeezed his trigger on impact, sending a bullet right through the partition and hitting Sosa in her face. The bullet entered her left cheek, grazed her tongue and exited out of her right cheek. She could literally taste the gunpowder mixed with blood in her mouth, and for a second she thought that she was dead.

The gunfire ceased and Semaj ran over and helped Sosa to her feet as they both looked down at the dead body of the most feared Jamaican in the world. He was a vicious murderer, an enemy to the Milano Family and the kidnapper of Sosa's daughter. Revenge was an understatement for what she was feeling inside. It was an overwhelming relief and fulfilling moment they both wanted to savor.

"We got to get out of here!" Vikingo yelled, snapping his fingers at Semaj and Sosa whose attention was fixed on Ox.

SWAT, FBI, ATF and local police entered the hospital locked and loaded. Some took the elevator and others took the stairs, but all reached the ICU Unit at the same time. Agent Flint led the FBI. He came down the hallway in a tactical manner with his gun out. SWAT got off the elevator and came down the hallway on the other side.

"We got an officer down!" Flint yelled as he passed Shark's partner who was lying in the hallway with a nurse tending to his wound.

They stormed the ICU and searched room after

room and checked the identifications of the nurses and doctors on the floor. There wasn't a crack or a crevasse in the unit that wasn't searched. After the whole floor was cleared, the only things that remained were two dead Jamaicans, another one alive but in critical condition, and a wounded cop.

Semaj, Sosa and Vikingo were nowhere to be found. Nor was Murda Mitch in his bed.

Columbia
One Year Later

The sun wasn't letting up. It was hot as hell outside and the bugs were biting Sosa's sweet skin as she crawled around on all fours. It had been a year since the shootout at the hospital, and during that time she had made somewhat of a life in Columbia staying on the compound with Semaj.

It wasn't until a few weeks ago that Semaj began to make her earn her keep there. It wasn't because she actually had to, but rather Semaj had something bigger in store for her.

"Now, explain to me why in the hell I'm out here in one hundred degree weather with nothing but a straw hat on for shade, picking weeds and planting seeds?" Sosa asked her while wiping the sweat from her forehead.

Semaj was sitting in a lawn chair sipping on a cold glass of lemonade "It's been a while since you got ya hands dirty, mama. Around here you gotta put ya own work in," she shot back.

Semaj had Sosa working the same coca field that Valentina had her working in when she first started. The same way that Semaj didn't understand, Sosa didn't understand either. But there was a method to Semaj's madness, and in the end it was going to benefit Sosa more than she could ever imagine. Right now, just like a flower she had to go through a little dirt before she could blossom.

Nyala too was enjoying the Columbian way of life, becoming more acquainted with the many children in her new family. The Espreilla family didn't have a problem taking in Sosa and Nyala and in the past year they grew to love them just as much as Semaj did.

The mini submarine surfaced in an undisclosed location in a river that ran through London. The Columbians that operated the machine didn't hesitate to unload the two tons of pure cocaine onto the banks. There wasn't a soul in sight for miles and that's how it was supposed to be. After every last brick was on land, the submarine submerged back under water, undetected by government sonar.

The cocaine sat there seemingly unattended, but it was being carefully watched until someone arrived to pick it up. Twenty minutes later three Range Rovers pulled up to the riverside. Murda Mitch jumped out of the truck and directed his boys to pick up the work, which they quickly loaded into the vehicles.

London was an open market since Qua moved his lucrative drug distribution back to the states and he was out of the picture, and what better person to take on the city than him. Murda Mitch was a well-known killer and had a crazy connect that would give him anything he wanted without paying up front. He was still a little weak from his injuries, but the team Semaj sent over with him was like no other. They took over the city by storm, and within a couple of months the people had adapted to his ways.

He stood there for a while looking out at the water and saw no signs of the submarine that his daughter sent the work over in. He just smiled and tossed a pebble into the water before returning back to the trucks after they had been loaded. He pretty much had London in the palm of his hands, and given time he would conquer all of Europe. But right now he had to supply London, and with his first big shipment of cocaine delivered he had more than enough to go around.

16 Tent Meeting, Australia

Nobody at the table said a word. They looked around at one another as they waited for someone to start the meeting. Usually it was someone from the Milano Family that headed the meetings, but their seats were empty. Nikolai looked like he wanted to say something, but every time he got to the edge of his seat in order to speak, confusion clogged his brain and he just sat back in his chair.

Semaj was the only one in the room who managed to crack a smile when Sosa high stepped into the tent, put her large Prada bag on the table and stood before the families. She normally wore baggy, non-stylish clothes, but today she was looking like a boss. She wore a cream Versace linen pants suit, a white silk blouse and a pair of tan Salvatore Ferragamo heels. Her hair was pulled back into a ponytail, and over her eyes were a pair of Prada shades. She was like a breath of fresh air, and Mrs. Naoroji had to nudge her husband in his ribs for looking at her so hard.

"Over fifty years ago, Marriano Milano brought our

families together under one roof," Sosa began. "Through the many years most of the original members have died and others were brought to life. I say this because many members of the Milano Family have died, but the family name must go on. I, Sosa Milano am here to represent the Milano Family and will do so until my time comes. The rules and regulations will remain the same and business will continue to be conducted in the same manner it has been throughout time. Now, before I continue this meeting, is there anybody here who objects?" she asked, looking around the room.

Nobody wanted to object, and frankly everybody was impressed with the way she addressed the meeting. It was professional, respectful and honorable, just like the Milano way. Not only was Sosa the boss of the Milano Family, she also was one of the biggest suppliers for the East Coast and most of the south. The only competition she had was Qua. He took the millions of dollars he made from London and brought his business back to the East Coast. Qua was still a legend in the streets and they welcomed him back with open arms.

"Now, because there are some new faces in the room I think it would be in order for us to introduce ourselves for the record. We can start from my right," Sosa suggested before taking a seat. Introductions were as usual. Nikolai, Wong Won, Marco Dedaj, Ezra Naoroji…

As everyone introduced themselves Semaj secretly hated the fact Qua had opted out of being a member of the 16 Tent and hoped that one day soon he would change his mind and come back. Although she let him go they still had unresolved issues to work out. Even after a year the love still wasn't gone. Semaj, who was already well known by everyone just waved her hand, motioning for the next person to go. She was a little arrogant but she had reason to be.

"You can call me Mitch. I represent the Richardson Family, now established in London," Murda Mitch announced and unbuttoned his Armani suit jacket.

With the help of Semaj, Mitch was the boss in London, and unlike the previous bosses the city had, the people actually liked him and the way he ran things. It was taking some getting used to, but Mitch was starting to enjoy the life of a boss, even though his main vocation was murder. But in time he had no doubt that he would get use to selling twenty-million dollars worth of cocaine a month. He had to. The Richardson Family depended on it.

When it got to the last family to introduce themselves, everybody turned their heads and waited for their response. It was a man and a woman, both who had stone cold looks on their faces. The man looked vaguely familiar to Semaj but she couldn't put her finger on who he was. She just sat quietly as the man got up from his chair, took a tote of his cigar and spoke.

"I'm Raul Ordonez, and this is my sister Salina Ordonez. We represent Cuba." The man looked around at everyone at the table, and then locked eyes with Semaj.

It didn't hit her at first, but as they stared at each

other for a moment the name and their faces reminded her of who they were. They were the siblings of Julio Ordonez, the disloyal Cuban that Valentina killed when Semaj visited her at her home.

He knew exactly who Semaj was and a billion dollar Drug Empire wasn't the only thing she had inherited. When Valentina died she left behind everything, including her beef. Hence the saying:

"MORE MONEY, MORE PROBLEMS!"

A KING PRODUCTION

Dior Comes Home...

*Rich
or
Famous*
Part 2

JOY DEJA KING

Lorenzo

Prologue

Lorenzo stepped out of his black Bugatti Coupe and entered the non-descript building in East Harlem. Normally, Lorenzo would have at least one henchman with him, but he wanted complete anonymity. When Lorenzo made his entrance, the man he planned on hiring was patiently waiting.

"I hope you came prepared for what I need."

"I wouldn't have wasted my time if I hadn't," Lorenzo stated, before pulling out two pictures from a manila envelope and tossing it on the table.

"This is her?"

"Yes, her name is Alexus. Study this face very carefully, 'cause this is the woman you're going to bring to me, so I can kill."

"Are you sure you don't want me to handle it? Murder is included in my fee."

"I know, but personally killing this back stabbing snake is a gift to myself"

"Who is the other woman?"

"Her name is Lala."

"Do you want her dead, too?"

"I haven't decided. For now, just find her whereabouts and any other pertinent information. She also has a young daughter. I want you to find out how the little girl is doing. That will determine whether Lala lives or dies."

"Is there anybody else on your hit list?"

"This is it for now, but that might change at any moment. Now, get on your job, because I want results ASAP," Lorenzo demanded, before tossing stacks of money next to the photos.

"I don't think there's a need to count. I'm sure it's all there."

"No doubt and you can make even more, depending on how quickly I see results."

"I appreciate the extra incentive."

"It's not for you, it's for me. Everyone that is responsible for me losing the love of my life will pay in blood. The sooner the better."

Lorenzo didn't say another word and instead made his exit. He came and delivered; the rest was up to the killer he hired. But Lorenzo wasn't worried, he was just one of the many killers on his payroll hired to do the exact same job. He wanted to guarantee that Alexus was delivered to him alive. In his heart, he not only blamed Alexus and Lala for getting him locked up, but held both of them responsible for Dior taking her own life. Lorenzo promised himself, as he sat in his jail cell, that once he got out, if need be, he would spend the rest of his life making sure both women received the ultimate retribution.

A King Production
Order Form

A King Production
P.O. Box 912
Collierville, TN 38027
www.joydejaking.com
www.twitter.com/joydejaking

Name: _____

Address: _____

City/State: _____

Zip: _____

QUANTITY	TITLES	PRICE	TOTAL
____	Bitch	$15.00	____
____	Bitch Reloaded	$15.00	____
____	The Bitch Is Back	$15.00	____
____	Queen Bitch	$15.00	____
____	Last Bitch Standing	$15.00	____
____	Superstar	$15.00	____
____	Ride Wit' Me	$12.00	____
____	Stackin' Paper	$15.00	____
____	Trife Life To Lavish	$15.00	____
____	Trife Life To Lavish II	$15.00	____
____	Stackin' Paper II	$15.00	____
____	Rich or Famous	$15.00	____
____	Bitch A New Beginning	$15.00	____
____	Mafia Princess Part 1	$15.00	____
____	Mafia Princess Part 2	$15.00	____
____	Mafia Princess Part 3	$15.00	____
____	Boss Bitch	$15.00	____
____	Baller Bitches Vol. 1	$15.00	____
____	Bad Bitch	$15.00	____
____	Princess Fever "Birthday Bash"	$9.99	____

Shipping/Handling (Via Priority Mail) $6.50 1-2 Books, $8.95 3-4 Books add $1.95 for ea. Additional book.

Total: $_____ **FORMS OF ACCEPTED PAYMENTS:** Certified or government issued checks and money Orders, all mail in orders take 5-7 Business days to be delivered.